When the Heart Remembers

Also by Constance Walker
in Thorndike Large Print ®

Warm Winter Love

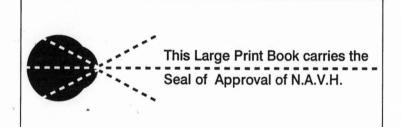

This Large Print Book carries the
Seal of Approval of N.A.V.H.

WHEN THE HEART REMEMBERS

Constance Walker

Thorndike Press • Thorndike, Maine

Thorndike Large Print ® Candlelight Series edition published in 1993 by arrangement with Thomas Bouregy & Co., Inc. Avalon Books.

The tree indicium is a trademark of Thorndike Press.

Set in 16 pt. News Plantin by Debra Ludden.

This book is printed on acid-free, high-opacity paper. ∞

Library of Congress Cataloging in Publication Data

Walker, Constance.
    When the heart remembers / Constance Walker.
      p.   cm.
    ISBN 0-7862-0043-X (lg. print : alk. paper)
    1. Man-woman relationships — Fiction. 2. Large type
books. I. Title.
    [PS3573.A425324W44   1994]
    813'.54—dc20   93-27243

For my mother and father,
Judith and Frank Cautilli,
with love

CHAPTER ONE

"I thought I recognized that voice from the long-ago distant past!" Sheilah put down the call-board on her desk and looked up at the good-looking but not-quite-handsome man and sighed. "Hello, Simon, what brings you here?"

Simon Kent grinned that lazy, half smile that millions of women watched and fell in love with every day on television. "Now, Sheilah, is that any way to greet an old friend?"

"Yes, if you're that old friend." Sheilah gave him an indulgent smile. "I ask you again, Simon, what are you doing here? I thought you were safely ensconced in Los Angeles at the station there. Or," she said, opening her gray eyes wide, "has California been swept away by a tidal wave?"

Simon arched an eyebrow and sat on the edge of her desk. "Ah, Sheilah, you're still letting your prejudices get the better of you. You always did think that the land of sunshine and orange juice ran a poor second to your East Coast concrete city streets."

She pointed a newly sharpened pencil at

him. "And you've forgotten all the blond sunshine girls that prejudice you, dear Simon."

"And you? You were always swayed by dark three-piece suits and striped ties." He looked down at his own navy suit.

"I liked patterns too." She shrugged. "I repeat, Simon, what are you doing here? You're not even one of us." She indicated the network letters on the wall.

"Not yet, anyhow, honey."

She winced at the word but ignored it. "Oh? Something I've missed?"

"You disappoint me, Sheilah. I was sure you were expecting me." He looked at her in one all-encompassing glance, taking in the beige-and-maroon silk dress, the beige jacket, and the creditable figure. "And here I thought you'd gotten dressed up especially for me." He walked toward the end of the hall. "See you." He waved as she watched his retreating back.

"Darn you, Simon Kent," she said under her breath. "I thought after five years you and I would never cross paths again."

She picked up her clipboard and penciled in some notes and grimaced just as Beth, her production assistant, brought in some letters.

"Was that —" she began, and Sheilah nodded.

"Uh-huh . . . Simon Kent, fellow journalist, master of the devoted daytime TV audience, winner of the Distinguished Newscasting Award, and the biggest rat you'll ever want to meet." She reached for a letter and began to read it.

"What's he doing here?" Beth asked. "He's great looking. Wouldn't it be nice to have something like him around here?"

"Close your mouth, Beth, and come back to earth," Sheilah said. "Simon Kent is just another pretty face in a long line of pretty faces on TV."

"Yeah, but wouldn't I like to take him home to Mother!"

"Be thankful, Beth, that you can't — if she's under eighty, he'd probably make a pass at her too." She signed the letter, handed it to Beth, and made a shooing motion at her. "Out, out, I've got a million things to do before the evening news and I don't want to stand around discussing the possibilities, real or imagined, professional or personal, of Simon Kent or anyone else."

Beth smiled at her and softly closed the door.

Sheilah began sorting through the manila folder filled with program notes and then looked up at the ceiling. *I wonder what he's doing here,* she thought. Could it really be

9

five years since she last saw him out in L.A.?
She shook her head. Beth was right . . .
he still did look good. She dialed Ben's office.
As director of on-air personnel, Ben Staud
would certainly know of staff changes.

"Hi, Sheilah, what's up?" His voice was
crisp, harried.

"Why's Simon Kent wandering our halls?"

"Is he here already? The board asked him
to come in and discuss a possible slot."

"I didn't know there was one."

"There isn't yet. It's all hush-hush, but
there probably will be. Another reshuffling
for ratings. Six o'clock's down by a point
— half a point — for the third month in
a row. Daytime looks pathetic . . . and upstairs is worried. We could use a big name
draw in the lineup. And 'Simon Says' is big."

"And so they're talking to Kent?"

"You got it. They found out his contract's
up in a couple of months, and they want
to see if he'll switch."

"Fat chance, Ben. Kent's a committed West
Coast type. Just mention the city and he
starts breathing as though he's choking on
exhaust fumes."

"How do you know so much about him?"
Ben's voice was interested.

"It's a long, tired story. I'll tell it to you
someday when you need to be bored."

"I'll hold you to it. Gotta go, Sheilah. Will I see you at the party?"

"Do I have a choice? Sure you will."

She held the receiver in her hand and tapped the mouthpiece softly against her lips. *So Simon's thinking of changing, is he?* She smiled to herself. *Well, at least I know he'll refuse to move here once he sees the city.*

It was noisy and crowded by the time she arrived at the office party. They were always the same. No real talk. She looked at the center table. The usual food — shrimp, Brie, Camembert . . . crackers, and those extra-special biscuits. She couldn't forget the biscuits. And the melon basket — maybe they'd have raspberries . . . no, they were out of season. But they had watermelon balls — just as good. She speared one with a colored toothpick, ate the pink fruit, and then put the used pick into an empty wine-glass that had been set on a windowsill.

Ben rushed past her. "Hold it," she said. "Nothing's happened yet. MacDonald's not here." She looked around. "It's too early. He'll probably make a grand entrance in a few more minutes."

"Sheilah," Ben said, exasperated, "when are you going to take this job seriously?"

"Me? Not serious? Listen, as long as I deliver on my end of the news, I figure I've

11

got the job. Right?"

"Yeah, you're right, of course. You're doing a great job on the eleven o'clock. Wish we could say the same about the early spot."

"Speaking of early shows . . . tell me about Simon Kent."

Ben backed away. "Some other time, Sheilah."

"Sure." She joined a group of account executives who stood talking among themselves. "Gentlemen, ladies — how goes it?"

Tommy, a portly, longtime station man, reached for her hand. "Come here, Sheilah, and talk to us. What's going on?"

"About what?"

"About Kent, naturally. You've heard he's here?"

"I've seen him."

"What's up? All kinds of rumors are going around. We account people are always the last to know."

"Come on, Tommy, that line won't work with me. You know you're usually the first to know. But this one beats me. I know about as much as you. Maybe," she answered, "he's here to discuss bringing his show to our station."

Tommy turned around and looked at her. "That's Ben Staud talk. He told me the same thing."

She shrugged. "But you and I know that's not right — he's not about to give up his West Coast base. So it looks as though we both really don't know anything."

So, she thought, *the rumor's around about Simon, is it? I wonder if there really is a possibility he'll be coming on board with us.* She looked out the window at the cold, gray sky. No, this wasn't his style . . . definitely not his style.

Ben stood beside her again. "Mac's coming now."

"Good, maybe then I can get out of here," she began and then saw Simon with the station owner. "Uh-oh, it's Mr. Wonderful."

"Come on, Sheilah, Mac's really a nice guy."

"I know that. I'm talking about Simon Kent."

"Say what you want, but we may be number one in the ratings yet."

"Yeah, maybe." She frowned. *Somehow, Sheilah girl, I don't like the way this is going,* she thought as she watched the two men. Mac was at his friendliest, and Simon, she saw, was at his all-time best — especially when speaking to the women on staff. She watched carefully as she saw them smiling . . . gesturing . . . eager to have Simon remember them.

The vultures! she thought. *Pretty soon they'll be finding ways to slip him their phone numbers.* She sniffed. *Oh, well, better them than me.*

MacDonald and Simon were walking toward her. She had to admit, he did look good. Hadn't aged a day, and that California tan still did wonders for him. She stared blatantly at Simon. He always did know how to dress . . . and his hair looked even better with that bit of silver in it. Wait until the people in the mailroom started getting those love letters to deliver. . . .

"Sheilah," MacDonald said as he approached her, "good to see you. I want you to meet Simon Kent."

She extended her hand and looked directly at the newcomer. "We know each other, Mac. Again, hello, Simon — how and why are you?"

Simon smiled that same slow, lazy grin. "Sheilah and I met a long time ago, Mac, when we both were breaking into TV. A real long time ago," he said as she gave him a dirty look. "Good seeing you again, Sheilah. See you around."

She raised her glass to him. "I'll drink to that." And then, as MacDonald and Simon left, she added under her breath, "Over my dead body, you will."

"He's really putting on a show for him,

isn't he?" Ben had once again appeared at Sheilah's side.

"What for? Kent's not the only one who could help us."

"Oh no? You know a bigger name or bigger draw right now? Or a hotter show than 'Simon Says'? He sure *can* help us, and he might just be available."

"Ben, not you too! The people in the accounts section are practically planning their sales pitches for their clients already. You can almost see them sharpening their pencils."

Ben looked at her. "I've never seen you like this before. What's gotten into you? You might think you've got something personal against the guy. He seems rather decent."

"That's because you're a man. Oh, forget it, Ben. It's just that I've had a long day on the phone trying to round up a feature." She touched his hand lightly. "It's only me being tired and grouchy. Forgive me."

Ben shrugged and walked away. "Sure. Whatever."

She took another sip of her wine while trying to decide whether she could slip away from the party unnoticed. Office parties were never her idea of fun, and she much preferred, especially on blustery nights like tonight, to be home reading a book or working a crossword puzzle. She twirled her glass, debating with herself whether she should stay another ten or twenty minutes.

"Hello again."

She jumped at the sound of the voice in her ear and smiled, still looking straight ahead, not turning toward him. "You don't faze me at all, Simon Kent. And if you think that whispering in my ear in the midst of all these people is going to make me blush, stammer, or go schoolgirlish on you, you can forget it. I'm grown-up now, my dear."

"I can see that. All those vitamins and minerals have finally fallen into all the right places."

She turned to face him. "And," she whispered as she half smiled, mindful of the people looking at her, "if you think that soft murmurings in my ear will cause me to fall madly in love with you, you're wrong again. One round of measles usually leaves you immune."

"Measles. Me? I always thought I was ptomaine poisoning."

She put her hand on his for a brief moment, patting it, still smiling so that the onlookers couldn't detect her words or intonation. "What are you doing here? Did you get on the wrong plane or something? Look over there," she said, pointing out at the New York skyline. "This is a city, and it's going to rain . . . you're going to get wet and ruin your perfectly styled haircut. Why don't you go back to California before it turns into a real downpour here?"

Simon started to laugh, a deep, delighted sound that pleased even her, and she began to laugh despite her resolve not to show any emotion.

"You really haven't changed, have you?" he asked, taking both her hands in his and looking her up and down. "Aside from being ten pounds — maybe fifteen — lighter, dressing a little more elegantly, and having shorter hair, you're still the inimitable Sheilah Godfrey! Ta-dah!"

"That's me, Simon. Gal/pal, writer, producer, and general all-around Ms. Understanding."

"That's good, Sheilah . . . misunderstanding, did you say?"

"Take that silly smirk off your face. That's a bad joke. Are you really going to take a job with us?" She stared directly into his eyes, demanding an answer.

"Whew!" he said, raising a hand as though to stop the questions. "When you go after an answer, you really go after it."

"You said I hadn't changed. And I was a darn good working reporter. Why won't you answer my question?"

"Why do you want to know?"

She looked down at her rose-enameled nails. "So I can pack my bags and take a long vacation or maybe just have enough time to buy an armor-plated heart."

Simon's smile faded, and for a brief moment there was a trace of seriousness in his voice.

"Would you need one?"

"No. Not anymore. But maybe you would. I'm sure working here with me you'll fall madly in love with me . . . again." She withdrew her hand from his. "Now, if you'll excuse me, it's late, and I've got to get home." She touched his shoulder very briefly. "Good-bye, Simon. Have a good stay here — not too long a one, but enjoy it."

He took her hand once more. "May I call you later?"

She hesitated, thought for a second, and then slowly shook her head. "No, Simon, I'd rather you didn't." She flashed him a dazzling smile. "Good night, and have a good flight."

She walked into the hall and began jabbing at all the elevator buttons. "Come on, come on!" she said impatiently. "I want to get out of here." The elevator door opened, and as she got into it she looked back at the entrance of the boardroom, where the party was still going on. She saw Simon watching

18

her. She smiled again and touched two fingers to her lips, and just as the door closed, she blew him a kiss that caught him unaware and surprised, and she started to giggle.

"That should fix him," she said, hunching her shoulders and going out the revolving door into the misty fall night.

CHAPTER TWO

The telephone rang just as she turned out the light beside her bed. "Hello?" she said sleepily.

"I never take no for an answer."

She caught her breath as she again recognized his voice. "You're right, Simon. I forgot that you can't accept it when someone says good-bye. Of course, there's no sense asking how you got my unlisted number."

"No," the smooth voice answered.

"Let me guess. You probably flashed that winning, hypnotic smile of yours at the night switchboard operator and she just melted. Am I correct?" She plumped the pillow behind her head and cradled the phone between it and her ear.

"That's the way it was, love. You always did know me so well." He exhaled a deep breath. "Tell me, did you really mean for us not to see each other again?"

"You do catch on quickly, Mr. Kent. I see you've learned something these past years. But then, time does wonderful things for egos. Anything else?"

"Yes, I just wanted you to be the first to know."

"Know what?" She sat up in the dark and switched on the light. "Know what?" she eagerly demanded.

"Thought that would get you. Now," Simon teased, "you're interested. Look, I know you're tired. Maybe I should just hang up."

"Simon!" she yelled into the phone loudly enough to awake Gatsby, her mixed-breed beagle, who was sleeping at the foot of her bed. "Don't you dare hang up before you tell me what you just called to tell me."

Simon's voice dropped down to a barely audible whisper, and she had to strain to hear him. "Are you sure you really don't ever want to see me again?" he asked.

"Yes."

"Then," he said, his voice getting even quieter, "fire your fairy godmother — she's asleep on the job. She's not going to grant you your wish. I've been offered a full hour a day, five days a week — count them, folks, that's five big ones — plus a Saturday rerun of my choice — at your station."

"No!" she yelled again. "Cut that out, Simon. Stop teasing. You can't take this job. You won't like it — it's not your territory — it's not your style —"

"You're my style."

"No, I'm not — you had your chance! But if you think you can scare me into getting upset, you're wrong. Good night, Simon. Enjoy your fun." She started to put down the phone, then added, "And listen, while you're out there, go play in traffic. Anywhere on Fifth Avenue will do." She hung up and turned out the light once more.

"Darn it!" she said after a minute. "That's it. No more sleep now." She got out of bed and walked to the window and sat down in a chair, looking out at the moonless night. Gatsby followed her, and she bent to pick him up.

"Why, after all these years, Gatsby, does he have to come back into my life? I'm doing well. I've forgotten completely about him and what he meant to me. I'm happy . . . successful . . . so why does he have to come back now?" She gently stroked the dog.

It was beginning to rain — her kind of weather — and she watched and listened as the sky lit up with a bolt of lightning and she heard the crack of thunder. Just as it struck, the phone rang again. "Don't tell me — another emergency at the station," she said aloud to the dog, who had raised his head. "Why can't emergencies wait until morning?" She spoke crisply into the phone. "Hello."

"Marvelous weather you have here in this city."

"No one asked you to stay. One more reason for you to fly away — fly away, Simon."

"Darn it, Sheilah, I'm standing here practically in the middle of Fifth Avenue and there isn't one cab in sight. And you call this civilization?"

"First of all, love, any real city person knows that cabs are hard to come by in this weather, so you make alternative arrangements — say, plan on getting home earlier . . . getting a friend to drive you. . . ." She looked into the mouthpiece of the phone. "Wait a minute, Simon . . . you don't expect me — tell me that's not the reason you called again." And then, hearing no reply, she added, "Simon, you really are something! I don't see or hear from you for five long years, and now you call me because you're stuck in the rain and need a ride! Forget it! Good night, Simon. I hope you drown." She slammed the phone down and smiled with mischievous satisfaction as another crack of thunder shook her closed windows.

The phone immediately rang again and

she knew it was him.

"Was it really five long years?" he asked softly.

"What?" She inhaled.

"I'm asking you if you thought it was really five long — emphasis on long — years since you've heard from me?"

"Yes, it was, but after the first week I began to like it that way."

"That's what I always admired about you, Sheilah, your soft, feminine ways. They were always absolutely charming."

"Charm's your department, not mine."

He started to laugh. "Enough. I call a truce. Okay?"

She could almost see his face in front of her, could almost see him touch the small zigzag scar just above his cheekbone, rubbing it unconsciously. Makeup and a different camera angle made it barely noticeable on TV.

"Stop rubbing it," she said.

"You remembered." His voice gave away his delight at her memory of his face and habits.

"Of course," she answered. "I remember all sorts of trivia. You should test me on geography — I'm a whiz. Want to know where South Dakota is — or maybe Duluth?" She glanced at the big luminous lucite clock above the mantel. "Simon, it's very late, and I have an early appointment tomorrow. Tell me just one thing. . . ."

"Anything, if you'll come and have a drink with me."

"No, the question's not important enough for me to lose my sleep and get soaked. I'll see you sometime." She started to hang up again and heard his voice as though from a distance.

"Wait! Sheilah, are you still there? Don't hang up — I haven't got any more quarters."

"I'm here."

"What's the question?"

"Are you really thinking about taking the job here?"

"Would you want me to?"

"Suit yourself."

"You've avoided the question," he said.

"So have you."

There was a silence. Then he said, "I'm thinking about it."

She leaned forward, her elbows on her knees, her left hand holding the phone. "Seriously?"

"Seriously . . . yes!"

There was another silence as she thought about her next question.

"Why, Simon?"

She was unprepared for his answer. "I'm getting bored."

She blinked. "You're joking. You never get bored."

"Well, maybe this time I am. Listen, Sheilah, how about that nightcap? For old times' sake?"

She looked out the window and saw the heavy torrent of rain cascading from the skies, hitting the window ledge with fat drops of water. She shivered and pulled her gown around her for extra warmth.

"I'll go for the rain check," she said, and they both laughed at her joke. "It's just a bit too wet out there."

"You wouldn't have to get wet."

"Of course I would," she countered, "even if I put on a raincoat and carried an umbrella." And then she tilted her head slightly and asked, "Where are you, Simon?"

"Downstairs in the lobby."

"The night switchboard operator again! Tell me, did she give you my social security number and blood type too?"

"Let's see . . . O negative . . . one, oh, eight, five, seven. . . ."

"You win. Give me five minutes to make myself decent and then come on up. I'm sure you know the apartment number." She hung up and shook her head. "Darn it,

Simon!" she said, getting her robe out of the closet. "Why do you have to be so likable?"

The bell rang just as she tied the pale-blue velour robe around her, and she opened the door. He was standing against the door frame, the shoulders of his suit jacket spotted with raindrops. He still looked as interesting and appealing as when he appeared on his TV program. He was smiling slightly, and there were little laugh lines formed around his eyes.

"Truce! You agreed," he said, offering her a bottle of red wine and a pot of bronze chrysanthemums.

"All right, truce. Where did you get these?" She took the flowers from him. Simon always had made her feel special.

"From the party."

"What?"

"Look, they kept me there until the end of the thing, and then they realized that I hadn't had anything to eat or drink, since I was so busy talking to everyone there. They wanted to take me out to dinner, but I said, 'No, just give me a bottle of wine and I'll go off and celebrate something with it.' And then I saw those chrysanthemums sitting on the table, and they reminded me of the time you and I went to the football game . . . remember? So I just grabbed them too."

"Didn't anyone say anything to you?" She put the gifts down on the cocktail table.

"No, I told them I had a great late date and I needed them to smooth the way."

She sighed. "Simon, you're preposterous! Suppose that I said no, that I didn't want to see you?"

"You didn't, though." He was close to her, and she could smell the lingering traces of his aftershave lotion. For a moment they both looked at each other, saying nothing, their eyes locked, and she felt her heart racing as though adrenaline had been pumped much too quickly into her veins. She saw the motion of Simon's hand moving closer to hers and then just as suddenly stopping.

"You're still a great-looking woman," he said, breaking the tension and stepping back.

"Thanks. Sit down, be comfortable. I'll just get some glasses."

She took a deep breath. *No*, she thought to herself. *I won't be intimidated. He may be charming and delightful, and he may tell me that I'm wonderful, but I will remember first and foremost that I want nothing to do with him ever again!* She reached for the glasses. "Never — never again!"

Simon walked toward her. "Did you say something?"

"I always talk to myself," she answered. "Ignore it."

"I always did!" he said under his breath but just loud enough for her to make out the words.

"Okay, hold it, Simon. I said a truce, not a chance to regroup for a coming war." She handed him the glasses and a corkscrew. "Here. It's your wine — you do the honors."

"Okay," he said, raising his palms to her in a gesture of defeat. "A truce is for civilized people, and we are — aren't we?" He deftly pulled the cork out of the bottle and poured the dark liquid into the glasses and handed one to her. "Here's to — what shall we drink to?" he asked her.

"How about a rainy night in New York City?"

"Okay," he agreed quickly, "to your kind of weather. Friend, here's to you." He touched her glass with his and took a sip.

"Now tell me about the offer. Who, what, when, where, how, and why?"

"You never forgot your reporting days, did you?" He leaned back against the cream linen cushions of the chair, and then, seeing her distrusting look, asked, "The who first?"

She nodded.

"MacDonald and a couple of others at the top heard that my contract's coming due in a couple of months and that negotiations with my station are at a standstill. In fact, we're not even close, my agent tells me." He took another sip of his wine.

She sat across from him on the matching cream couch, her feet tucked under her, the hem of her robe curled under them. "Go on."

"Well, someone from here — Gretel Dorn, I think it was — put out some feelers —" He stopped as she made a face, scrunching up her nose and mouth. "What's the matter?"

"Oh, nothing, but I'll just bet it was Gretel. She's been itching to get somebody good looking on board so she could get her hooks into him."

"Oh? You still consider me good looking?"

"Stop playing coy, Simon. It doesn't become you. Of course you're good looking — although a little older than last time I saw you. But, like good cheese, you've aged fairly well. You know it. You have a mirror, don't you? Just go on."

"Well, Gretel put out these feelers —"

She arched her eyebrows. "So now it's Gretel? My, you two must have gotten on famously!"

"You want to hear this or not?"

"I'm fascinated. Yes." She wriggled her toes.

"Gretel approached my agent and asked if I would be interested in speaking with her and her station. My agent said no harm in that and even told me later that having it around that some other stations were interested would be a good bargaining chip for me. And WBSW is no low-man-in-the-rating-poll station! So I spoke to a couple of people — MacDonald, for one, when he was out on the Coast for a convention — and they asked me to fly in this week for more negotiating. Harvey, my agent — you remember him, don't you?"

She nodded. "He's still with you?"

"Sure. We always got along great. Well, anyway, Harvey didn't want it to be too much of an overkill on our part, so he asked MacDonald to try and keep the talk down to a decent roar."

"That's what you call tonight — a decent roar?"

"MacDonald arranged the party. Not us. Anyway, here I am."

"That's a beginning." She leaned back. "Go on."

"You really are something, you know? How could anyone look so efficient in the newsroom and so thoroughly lovable at home

and still come on like some — some —"
He groped for a word.

"Let's see." She turned her head. "A few years ago you called me a tough broad. Will that do?" She held out her glass for a refill.

"For want of a better phrase. Well," he said, taking the glass from her, "evidently, the powers that be here at the station were more than ready to offer me the spot — and to meet me halfway on the changes I wanted if I came on board."

"What changes? No one's talked about anything new."

"They will," he said seriously, "if I come here." He handed her the wineglass.

"We'll talk about that later," she said.

"Okay," he continued, "now we're up to the when. Looks like they want to go with the same format — do a live show in the morning, just before the soaps — and as soon as possible. So if I accept and Harvey and the lawyers can work things out, including a network syndication clause — and a hefty raise, which, by the way, I know I deserve —"

"You probably do," she conceded.

"— it would be about the middle of October, give or take a week. The next question — where? — you know. It's here in Studio A — or is it B? The how — simply by packing my bags, signing a contract, and that's it."

"You forgot the why!" She put a finger against her mouth and bit the nail. "Tell me about the why."

"Ah, the why!" He swung his arm from over the back of the chair. "That's the most difficult part to answer," he said with unexpected honesty. He looked directly at her, and she once more felt her heart beating faster as she noticed how his brow wrinkled in thought and a small smile played around the corners of his mouth. Finally, he pressed his lips together, shook his head, and said, "I honestly can't answer that."

She narrowed her eyes. "Will they let you go so easily?"

"If you're asking me am I secure in my job in California, the answer is yes. I know they'll come to my terms — eventually. We all know that 'Simon Says' is great stuff and a draw, but — it's just —" He shrugged his shoulders. "It's just that maybe I wasn't kidding when I said I was getting bored out there. Maybe it *is* time for me to pack up and try something new . . . someplace different."

"It'll be the same here. Same news . . . same people . . . same audience . . . only in a different city. You know everything's always the same. Only the names and faces and locations change."

"Yeah, but maybe that's what I need."
Then, in an abrupt change that she remembered was always consistent with his moods, he laughed and added, "And then again, maybe all I need is a good night's sleep and a chance to see all this concrete in the daytime."

She swung her legs from the couch to the floor and started to rise. "Maybe," she said, "and maybe not. But I'm warning you, Simon, you'd better take a long hard look before you make a move."

"Speaking of moves," he said, gesturing around him, "you've done quite well for yourself here. I like it."

"So do I — I've always been an art deco fan."

"Yes, I remember."

"You do?" She was surprised and touched at his memory. "Well, thanks for the flowers and the wine."

"Thanks for giving a stranger refuge for an hour or so." He reached out toward her, and she tensed, half hoping at the same time that he would and wouldn't hold her. But instead he brushed away a stray wisp of hair that had fallen across her cheek. The sudden, casual touch of his hand against her face disturbed her.

He opened the door. "Well, Sheilah, if I don't see you again — you . . . you still look sensational!" He touched his fingers to his forehead in a mock salute and then quickly pulled the door shut.

She stood looking at but not seeing the closed door, and she shivered and pulled her robe tighter around her, knowing that the trembling wasn't from the cold.

"Oh, Simon!" she said, feeling Gatsby nudge against her foot. "Oh, Simon, I wish — I wish you'd never come back into my life. Please don't take the job." But she knew that somehow she really wasn't being honest asking for that wish.

CHAPTER THREE

Beth handed Sheilah a stack of newspapers. "Is he really coming on board?" she asked.

Sheilah shook her head. "Why ask me? I really don't know. But what I do know is that we'd better get busy or there won't be an eleven o'clock news-feature show tonight. What about the interview with that diet-book author? Were you able to get her?"

"Sure, no problem. I'll get you the info sheet on her. She's talkative, so she'll make a good guest."

Sheilah turned to the TV section of the paper.

"The third paragraph," Beth said. "It's already in the papers — that he may come with us."

"I don't care, Beth. We've got work. Get me that bio sheet, will you?"

Sheilah leaned on her desk. *I wonder,* she thought, *if he's gone back to the Coast yet. And what he's going to do.* She pushed back her chair and got up and walked around the room, her high heels coming down hard into the gold carpeting.

He'd be great for the station, but he wouldn't

be for me! she mused. *No, definitely, he wouldn't be good for me.* She kicked at the carpeting. If he took this job, what would happen to them . . . to her? She sat down again at her desk. *Sheilah Godfrey,* she said to herself sternly, *don't forget this is the original golden boy you're talking about. Sunshine and surf and Simon go together. Forget it . . . he'll never take the job.*

MacDonald announced the news at the next weekly staff conference. "All the rumors you've heard, I'm glad to say, are definitely true," he said as Sheilah sat down at the opposite end of the conference table. "Simon Kent has signed with us." He looked at everyone. "There won't be any immediate changes in our programming schedule. As you know, we were looking for a different format for the morning, and 'Simon Says' is it. You all know the popularity and the ratings of the show, and I'm really pleased to tell you that Simon will be with us soon. And I don't mind telling you that the thought of giving the other stations a run for their money genuinely excites me — as it should all of you."

"It'll be nice to have the ratings go up," Ben whispered to Sheilah.

"They'd better! Or all this will have been

in vain." She recognized the hard edge to her voice.

Ben gave her a curious look as they left the meeting. "How come you're so unhappy about Kent coming on board?"

"It shows, huh?" She stopped walking. "Tell me, Ben, would you be upset if you had someone brought into your department and you didn't know how that person would affect your job? Especially if that person had been hailed as the ultimate personnel manager?"

"Probably, but I think you're being too uptight about all this. It shouldn't affect your position."

"It shouldn't?" She looked at him. "Are you kidding?"

"No, it's not *your* show that's going to be affected. We'll still need local news features for the news. Simon's national — *international* — and you're local. Big difference."

"Ah, but that's just the point — ten to one Simon Kent will get anything his little heart wants, because he is — what shall we call him — global? Already I can see him getting the star treatment. So, what happens to my show — my budget? Will it be cut to accommodate him?"

"Hey, hold it. One, Simon's going to use

the same budget that was programmed for at least three months. Two, no personnel changes for at least three months, until we can see where we are and where we're heading. Three, no star treatment — that's his request, he really doesn't want it. And four, and most important, what the heck is really bugging you about him?"

"Does it show that much?"

"From about a mile away. I know you're not jealous of him — you're not the type — so that's really a smoke screen. You're not worried about career problems — you're too talented and you're moving up. And since I'm a pretty fair personnel director, I'd say it was more than that. I'd say it was a personal problem." He took off his glasses and wiped the lenses. "Am I right? Sheilah, the way you're acting, I'd hazard a guess and say either you dislike him intensely or there's something between the two of you."

"You really are pretty good at reading people. There *was* something . . . in the past. I was in love with him once. And now, after all these years . . . I don't know what I feel about him."

Ben tapped his foot on the floor. "Look, I'm a pretty good listener. Want to have dinner with me this evening? Ginger's out of town."

"Ginger? The dancer you introduced me to last year?"

Ben smiled. "Who else? I can't resist her. You don't think I spend all my days and nights thinking about WBSW, do you?" He took her hand. "Come on — you need a friend to talk to, and I need a person to eat with."

It was a slow night at the restaurant, and the waiter promptly served them dinner. "Okay," she said in between forkfuls of pasta, "it's a long story — I'm warning you."

"It usually is. Go on — I'll tell you when I'm bored."

"Well, you're right. I knew Simon about six years ago — before I took this job. I worked out in California for a while. I was an assistant producer — although I began as a gofer at a small station. I moved up, got an on-camera reporting job, went on to a producer's job at the station, then moved on to a little larger outfit . . . but you know all this, it's in my résumé."

"Uh-huh. Where does Simon fit into all this?"

"I met him at WFAC — he had a local show, and we met each other, and —" She put her fork down. "And one thing led to another, and I fell in love with him. I thought he felt the same way, but I was wrong.

40

Simon didn't want one person — for him, it's the more the merrier — and I decided I couldn't compete for him and still compete in the workplace. So when you people made me an offer and Simon didn't resist or even get upset — didn't even care, actually — I figured I'd had it with the land of sunshine and avocados, and I headed back here."

She speared an avocado slice onto her fork and waved it at Ben. "I used to eat these things right off the trees — now I raise the plants from seeds on my kitchen windowsill."

"And you still don't know what you think of him."

"For a long while I hated him. But after I moved I never heard from him again, so the hate faded, and I thought there was just a patch over the hole in the part of my heart where Simon had been."

"Now you're not so sure." He leaned back in his chair.

"No. I hadn't heard from him in all these years — not even a postcard — until he walked in here last week. Of course, I heard about his phenomenal success, and I really think his show deserves it. It is good, but —"

"Will you be able to work with him?"

"With him?" She opened her eyes wide. "*With* him?"

41

"Not with him directly. I mean in the same building . . . in the next studio?"

"Oh. I think so. If you mean will I sabotage him or create problems — no, I'm too professional for that."

"I know that. I didn't think of it that way."

She picked up his hand and squeezed it. "You really are a great friend, Ben. Enough about me and Simon Kent — let's change the subject. Tell me about Ginger. . . ."

The next morning Beth rushed into Sheilah's office, eager to tell her boss the news.

"You should see what they're doing down the hall." Beth's eyes shone. "New carpeting, new chairs and desk — even a couch. It's going to be sensational."

"Beth," Sheilah said, looking up from her schedule sheet, "it's called the all-out treatment. Don't you remember your childhood game — whatever Simon says, you do, and in this case, they're doing!"

"I wouldn't mind saying 'May I?' to him."

"Enough! So Simon Kent is coming aboard. Simon Kent is not on our show. We have a show — remember?"

Her assistant shrugged. "Well, he *is* gorgeous, even if you don't think so."

"Did I say he wasn't attractive? He's perfectly marvelous — he's charming — but that still isn't going to get my work done. I'm really tired of hearing about this great person who's coming to save our station. Okay, that's it." She got up and poured herself a cup of coffee from the plugged-in percolator on the small table. "Oh, forget it, Beth. It's been a rough day, that's all."

"No matter." Beth went back to her own desk.

Sheilah put a fingernail to her lips and bit down on it. "Oh, Simon, why did you take this job?"

Three weeks later she heard his voice again.

"Hiya, sweetheart."

"Be still my heart!" She raised her hand to her chest. "Don't tell me — the whole world's been expecting him — it must be the displaced Californian." She grinned at him. "Or," she continued, "it's the voice of the ghost of television past. No wonder they call it the boob tube." She extended her hand to him. "No matter, I promised myself and Personnel that I would be on my best behavior. So, welcome, Simon, your subjects await you."

Simon smiled that lopsided grin again and waved his hand in Sheilah's direction. "Naughty, naughty, Sheilah. I thought you said you were going to be nice."

"I only said it — I didn't have to mean it." She pulled a chair next to her desk. "Come on in. I'll even offer you a cup of coffee by way of a peace offering and a welcoming gift."

He sat down. "You were always all heart, love, as I remember."

"Forget it, Simon. And don't call me 'love.' And do yourself a favor and forget the re-membering routine. From now on you'll be judged by your merits here." She poured a cup of coffee. "Black, wasn't it?"

He took the mug and put it down on the desk. "I see you remembered that."

"No, purely a guess. Most of the people I know take it black, or mean to — diets, you know."

He looked her up and down slowly, and she shifted uncomfortably and sat down, tuck-ing her skirt closer around her.

"You still have a gorgeous pair of legs."

"You do too." She grinned again. "Now I'm *really* flattered you remembered — what with all the gorgeous legs I'm sure you've seen."

Simon burst out laughing. "You know, Sheilah, this may be fun — working with you again."

"Fun? Why?"

"Because you're still the lovely, witty, charming person I remember from all those halcyon days we shared."

She raised an eyebrow and fixed Simon with a stare. "My, my . . . I never thought you looked upon those West Coast days as the highlight of any time. Frankly, Simon, I find them difficult to remember."

"Selective memory, eh?"

"What?"

"Nothing, love. Oops, sorry." He swallowed the rest of the hot coffee and stood up. "Sheilah, I'd love to spend more time recapturing the good old days, but duty calls." He picked up a newspaper off her desk.

"It was in last week's paper, Simon — the blurb about your coming to work for us. If I'd known you collected your own press clippings, I would've saved them."

"They could be valuable someday."

"So it's true — you *do* believe your own press image." She nodded. "Welcome, Simon, nice seeing you again."

"I get the message." He started for the door, and then turned. "You know, for a TV producer, you still have a great pair of legs." He laughed and softly closed the door.

She didn't see him for several days, and she knew management was spending time with him working out the fine details of his

45

position at the station.

So far so good, she said to herself while she looked for tapes of prior broadcasts. *As long as he stays out of my show and my life, this will work.* She pulled out a drawer and saw empty spaces where the reels had been stored.

"Beth, why are some of the tapes missing? I can't find that piece on fire safety."

"Oh, I thought you knew." Beth looked up from the TV monitor. "Gretel asked me to get some of them to show Simon — he wanted to see what we'd produced and what kind of interviewing we'd done on the news programs."

"Gretel told you to do that! Since when do you take orders from her? You're supposed to be *my* assistant. And she's supposed to ask *me* about my show." She stopped the editing machine. "What did you do with them?"

"Gave them to Simon, like she asked. Gee, I'm sorry if I caused any trouble."

"No, forget it — I'll clear it up. Don't worry," she said, hurrying down the hall.

The door to Simon's office was closed, and she knocked once and went in without waiting for him to acknowledge her.

"Look, Simon," she began, and saw that both he and Gretel were sitting on the leather couch in front of the window, TV logs spread out before them. Gretel held a pencil, and her hand remained in mid-air as she looked up and saw Sheilah.

"Hi," Simon said, oblivious to her anger, "be with you in a minute."

"This isn't a friendly call —"

"Hello, Sheilah," Gretel said in the perfectly controlled voice that always angered Sheilah. "We were just talking about you."

"I'll just bet you were. Look, Simon," she began again, "I don't mind your wanting something from my show — only just ask me, will you, and not her." She pointed at Gretel. "She's not in charge of my tapes — she's in programming and in charge of a lot of things, but definitely not my show or my property!" Her eyes flashed at the other woman. "You don't have the right to tell my assistant or ask my assistant for anything — and especially not for my tapes." She turned to Simon. "Just ask me, okay, and I'll get you whatever you need. But just ask *me!*"

"Wait a minute, Sheilah." Simon's voice took on a conciliatory edge. "I didn't ask for those tapes — Gretel volunteered them."

"Gretel volunteers a lot of things."

He ignored the remark. "And when I said I wanted to know what you'd already done,

47

she said why not look at your shows. It sounded reasonable." He looked over at Gretel, who was sitting demurely on the couch, buffing a nail.

"That's right, Sheilah. I told him about the wonderful things you were doing, and then I guess I must have overstepped my boundary and volunteered them for him. I did want Simon to see what you were capable of doing on your show."

She glared at Gretel. "Capable of doing?" Her voice rose to an edge.

"Well, perhaps that was the wrong word. . . ."

"You bet it was."

Gretel stood up, smoothed her purple suit skirt, and walked to the door, taking the program logs with her. "I'll be going, Simon. I have another meeting." She smiled at him, slightly closing her carefully made-up brown eyes. "I will see you later, won't I?"

"Yeah, sure." He nodded.

Sheilah heard the door click behind her.

"I will be seeing you later, won't I?" Sheilah mimicked.

Simon shook his head. "Okay, Sheilah — want to tell me what that was all about?"

"Sure. You've just witnessed about three minutes' worth of a stand-up comedy routine — 'The Gretel and Sheilah Hour,' they call it around here — flare-ups for all occasions. What do you mean, what was that all about?" She kicked at the floor. "Oh, I don't know." She ran her dust-spotted hand through her hair, pushing back a strand that had crossed her side part. "I'm just uptight, that's all." She sat on the edge of his desk.

"Do you always get this violent about missing tapes?"

"No. It's just that woman."

"Gretel?"

"Oh, don't play cute with me, Simon. Of course, Gretel. She's the biggest man-eating she-shark in the whole place. She gives every woman a bad name."

Simon pointed an index finger at his chest. "And you think she's after me?"

"Does it matter?"

"You tell me — I'm interested." His eyes caught hers for just a moment, until, rattled, she glanced away.

"You think I'm jealous of her? Of *her?*"

"Maybe."

"You've spent too much time in the sun, Simon. Of course I'm not jealous of her. It's just that every time I see her 'I'm so wonderful' face I want to throw up. And then when Beth told me how she commandeered my shows. . . ."

"It was an honest mistake — mine, really.

49

But I just didn't want to duplicate anything you'd done or anyone you'd interviewed in the past year. Gretel suggested I look over your stuff. You can understand that, can't you? Honestly, there was no conspiracy." He touched her arm gently, and although it was only a friendly gesture, she was aware of its warmth. She got up and started to walk around the office.

"I know. I guess I really knew it, but darn it, I don't like people going into my files without asking." She sat on the leather couch and crossed her legs. "I guess I'm just jumpy."

"The awards?"

"You've heard! I never could understand why stations put so much store in whether they win or lose awards. Half the time it's really political . . . or a personality contest."

"Yeah, but you've got to play the game."

"That's just it. I'm tired of playing the game. Why don't they just judge people on their own merit?"

"Don't ask me. I don't know. I think sometimes that my best stuff goes unrecognized and they give me a nomination only for my interviews on controversial subjects and people."

She looked at the walls of Simon's office

and saw framed citations. "You're a fine one to be asking — look at all this stuff. What'd you do — start collecting them when you were six?"

"Still as mercurial as ever, aren't you? Just when I think you're calming down, up goes the temperature charts and — bango! — I step onto another land mine."

She pounded her right hand into the fist of her left hand. "I guess I never learned to shut my mouth. I either put my foot into it or end up eating my words. Sorry about that." She picked up the file tape on Simon's desk. "This mine?"

"Yes. You've got some pretty good stuff there."

"Ah, rare praise from the exalted one." She snapped her fingers. "There I go again. You'll have to forgive me, Simon. I need a vacation. I've been working too hard."

"I can tell." He grinned. "Let me take you away from all this. I can't offer you a vacation, but how about dinner this evening? At least work will be off your mind for a few hours." He again unconsciously touched her arm, and she smiled.

"Sure, why not? As long as you promise not to talk shop, make a pass, or talk about old times."

"Okay." He sounded playful. "If you'll

go along with my conditions, too."

"Which are?"

"It'll be dinner as long as you promise not to talk shop, make a pass, or talk about old times."

She took a deep breath and relaxed her shoulders.

"Ah, Simon, you still can make me laugh."

"Good. I'll see you about eight o'clock." Again the smile, and she bit her lip. *Oh, Simon,* she thought, *what makes you so charming? And what makes me so vulnerable?*

CHAPTER FOUR

Simon looked around the small Afghan restaurant decorated with wall hangings and tall potted plants. "This place reminds me of all those little restaurants we used to discover back —"

"No, Simon," Sheilah interrupted, "old times are taboo, remember? It's today — now — that counts."

"Whatever you say. Well, what shall we talk about? You — me — the world?" He leaned forward and reached for her hand, but she quickly pulled it away and picked up her napkin.

"Dinner. Let's talk about dinner."

"Okay." He motioned toward her hand, which now held the unfolded napkin. "That was a pretty deft move, by the way."

"Lots of practice."

"I can tell. Well, food it is — is it good?"

"Yes."

He nodded his head in agreement and laughed. "Okay," he said slowly, "next topic. Come on, Sheilah — can you imagine you and me having to put restrictions on what we say to each other?" He reached once again for her hand, and this time he held it. "Let's just talk." He looked around the room once more. "Do you remember that time we met that weird old man who was dressed in those black clothes?"

"The one you thought was Jack the Ripper?"

"Not me. It was you who kept insisting that we get out of that place. I wasn't afraid of him — I just thought he was a little strange."

"Then why'd you duck when he reached inside his pocket?"

"I thought he was going to pull out a knife — or a gun —"

"And all it was was a letter he had written to the station suggesting that we have more old murder mysteries on the late, late show. He had recognized you from your news show. You know," she said, glancing down at the table, "that was the fun of working out there, Simon. I have to admit there were some good times."

"Of course there were — there usually are. You create them. How about here?"

"Oh, about the same. I really didn't mislead you about that. The station's a little more uptight — the people are more tense — but sometimes that's good. At least it is for me. I like the competition and the challenge."

She tilted her head.

"I had forgotten how lovely you look by candlelight." He said it simply, without warning, and she looked at him across the flickering flame, suddenly feeling uncomfortable for the first time that evening.

"Simon, let's not spoil it now. We're just beginning to be easy with each other — let's not muddy it up with rememberings."

"Okay, but —"

"No buts."

"Your choice, Sheilah." He sipped his wine. "Tell me about your job."

"It's interesting — and rewarding. Doesn't that sound trite? Like something you'd find on a résumé? But it really is. I'm pretty much in control and doing what I want here — and I can get people for the news whom I think would fit in." She put down her fork. "Not just airheads or glamour people. I can get politicians up here even when they're not running for office, or local people who just want to say something about how life is in their neighborhood.

"That's the fun part for me, Simon, talking to all those people. Sort of what you do, only where you have an hour to go into depth, I have sixty- or ninety-second blocks peppered throughout the news. If you remember, my philosophy of the news was that what made the small towns run was the same sort of stuff that makes the big cities work." She smiled. "I've wanted to do this for a long time."

"I don't think I've ever seen that spark — that alive look you just had when you explained your job." He slapped the table, and she felt a warmth rush over her face. She tossed her head, hoping the gesture would cool her.

"I talk too much sometimes. Your turn," she said.

"What about me? I'm still the same old Simon you knew."

"Oh, no, that's not true, and you know it. You've come a long way."

"We both have."

"Not like you — you're phenomenal!"

"Yeah, I've had some good luck." His fingers caressed her hand. "Do you ever think of the old days — of us?"

"Simon!"

"Let me at least ask the question."

"That was five years ago . . . it's history."

"I know, but I just wondered."

"Don't. Don't ask me questions like that. You're very good at interviewing, and I might say something I don't want to." She was playful, hoping to change the mood.

"I wouldn't dare. You're too smooth for

me — you evade questions too skillfully."

"So do you — you always did."

His voice was mock indignant. "I never hedge questions. I answer as honestly as I can."

"Since when?" She was enjoying the contest.

"Always." He jutted his jaw.

"Always? No way, Simon, this is Sheilah you're talking to. Remember?"

He leaned closer to the center of the table; the candlelight reflected off the shiny, small scar on his face, and she had to look away in order to avoid forbidden memories.

"Try me. Go on, ask me any question and I'll answer."

"No evasions?"

"No, I'll answer anything. Go on," he challenged, "ask me anything."

"Who's buried in Grant's Tomb?"

"Edgar H. Grant. He broke the record swimming the Pacific Ocean. Try another."

She started to laugh. "Who's Chaucer?"

"The guy who invented the dish that goes with a cup."

She giggled.

"No, don't stop now," he said, "you've got me on a roll. Ask me a harder question."

"Who says, 'moo, moo'?"

"A Hawaiian woman buying a dress. Quick. Faster, faster."

"Why didn't you call me after I left?" She whispered it and then gasped, horrified that she had spoken too quickly, too caught up in the silliness of the mood. He dropped her hand in surprise. "No, don't answer that. I don't even know why I asked that question."

"I didn't know your number." His voice was even, serious, and his tone cut through her, causing a stabbing feeling in the pit of her stomach so that she unconsciously pulled at her belt.

"You could have looked it up." She looked down, embarrassed. "Enough!" Her voice had become distant, businesslike. "See what happens when I dawdle over my food and drink wine?" She gestured toward the empty plate in front of her.

"Yes." He accepted her excuse readily, and they both watched silently as the waiter cleared the table.

"Let's try again," she said. "Talk to me about your plans for your show. It's going to be the same, isn't it?"

"Sure, that's why they hired me. And, like you, I like what I do. I like asking people questions about what makes them or their causes tick. That's what I'm all about."

"I know."

"You do?"

"Why are you so surprised? I knew you,

I was interested in you — and I'm always interested in what people are doing in this business. I know that once you started your show, you rose quickly. Right to the top. But I always knew you would. I never expected you to end up as just a local anchorman." She smiled nervously. "When you first started 'Simon Says' the public was right out there with you. You were — and are — just what they want. You ask the questions people want to ask. You're one of them! That's what makes you so good."

"I had no idea you were paying attention, Sheilah."

"I couldn't help but follow your career. How could anyone who ever watched TV not know who or what you are? You've done really well, Simon — some good interviews. That one on kids and drugs was super. Everyone talked about it — the fact that you were one of the first to bring experts, kids, and parents together on a show. It was a great idea." She ran her finger down the side of her water glass.

"Yeah. I just figured we couldn't talk without each of the groups being represented, and I got lucky — before all the publicity — and had some people who were willing to talk openly without yelling and screaming and placing blame."

"It was a hit. Look at the bundle of awards you picked up for that show."

Simon put down his spoon. "You surprise me. I was sure that after you left California you'd never have wanted to hear from — or about — me."

"That's unfair. I've always tried to separate my personal life from my professional one, and no matter what I personally think about you — about us — I can't deny that you're a good interviewer. You're talented. You know that!"

Simon shook his head, and she continued, "Why are you puzzled? Because I'm truthful? I always was — that's what got me into constant trouble."

"Don't I know you were always truthful! But you're right, I am puzzled. I wonder why you never told me all this when we were out there in California . . . together."

"Probably because I was jealous and scared."

"What?" Simon's hand had started for his water glass but stopped in mid-air. "You, jealous? Of what?"

She wrinkled her brow, thinking, then looked back into Simon's direct gaze. "Of you — of your success, of the fact that I might have been considered a hanger-on, of failing where you'd succeeded, of a dozen things. Name anything and then take your choice." She fingered her napkin.

"Hey — wait a minute. This is Sheilah, isn't it?"

"See? That's just what I mean." She cocked her head at him. "That's what everyone thought of me — good old Sheilah — not Sheilah Godfrey, producer. Just good old Sheilah, Simon's girlfriend. I don't think anyone at the station, including you, ever realized how afraid I was of not making the grade — how I wanted — no, how I *needed* — to be told that I was doing really well. No one ever thought of me as anything but strong and — and Simon's girl."

"Oh, wait a minute. You were being upped the ladder. You were being promised things."

"Promises, Simon, from everyone. Even you. But nothing ever materialized. That producer's job on the early news? It went to someone else! The spot on the noon interview show? Someone else got it! I never knew whether I was at the station merely to mollify Simon Kent into not bolting his contract or — or — for what!"

"You mean you thought you were the lure that held me there?" He shook his head, astonished. "You can't mean that!"

"Yes, I could, and I did. You know, Simon, no one ever looked at me — *really* looked

61

at me. No one even considered the possibility that I needed some support. Not even you."

Simon continued to shake his head slowly. "I didn't know, Sheilah. I really didn't know. You never said anything, never even let on about your feelings. You kept it all hidden."

"I had to. There was no one to tell it to." She picked up her cup and finished the last of her coffee. "No one was really interested in me or my feelings or my career."

"And that's why you ran?"

"Ran?" She shifted in her chair. "I not only ran, I practically won the Olympics when I was given the opportunity to move up and away. Wouldn't you have if you had been me?" She put her elbows on the table and extended her hands toward him, palms up, close to the pink flowers and candle in the center of the table. "Reverse the situation, Simon. I'm making it big — or at least the promise is there — and you're still who and what you are when you first got to the station, only you're known as Sheilah's guy. Tell me what would you have done. Tell me how fast you would've skipped town."

Simon crinkled his eyes so that little creases appeared in the corner. He nodded his head. "You're absolutely right! I would have gotten the heck out of there if they'd offered me a show in Podunk. I would have taken any-thing."

She smiled, a full, wide smile showing the slightly uneven edge of her upper teeth against the almost worn-off coral lipstick. "Thanks."

"For what?"

"For being honest with me. You know, I've tried explaining all this to myself a hundred times, and each time I kept thinking, well, maybe I hadn't played it right. Maybe I was wrong to have gotten out. Not that I need your confirmation now — no, it's more than that. What I wanted was for some-one else to understand what I did and why I did it."

"There's only one thing I don't under-stand."

"What's that?"

"Why didn't you tell me? What made you think you couldn't tell me all this when you were feeling it?"

"Would you have really understood? Would you have listened to me? We were both so caught up in our own things and our own careers that neither of us was much good at understanding."

"That's a harsh indictment of me, don't you think?"

"I'm indicting myself too. I admitted that

I wouldn't have cared about you."

"Maybe so. But speak for yourself! I'm not sure that I like your putting your thoughts into my head. You should have at least tried explaining to me."

"Why?" She was belligerent.

"Hey, wait a minute. I recognize that tone in your voice — I used to hear it a lot, remember? Let's back off. This is supposed to be a fun evening. No conflicts — no nothing."

"We broke the rules about two hours ago."

"We'll just reinstate them." He watched as she arranged and rearranged the salt and pepper shakers until they finally were back to their original positions.

"Why should I have told you I was unhappy?"

"It might have worked out."

"Really? How?"

"We were supposed to be friends."

"That was just it, Simon. We were supposed to be *more* than friends. But you kept running around — all those women. I kept thinking, 'Well, this will pass too,' but there was always another woman waiting around the corner for you. We were supposed to have had some sort of a commitment."

"Hey, I never said that."

"No, not in so many words. But your actions?"

"Oh, no — no way. At that point in my life I knew I wanted no strings — no ties — no commitments. My profession had to come first. I thought you understood that."

"I guess I just expected that since you were spending so much time with me. . . ."

"Much time, yes, but not all of it. You remember — you even said I was running around a lot. Sure I was. And you were free to do as you chose. I knew I had no hold on you."

"But you knew I wasn't going out with anyone else."

"Hey!" Simon spread his hands out in front of him. "There you go again, trying to insert your thoughts into my head. I didn't know who you were seeing or if you were seeing anyone else. What you chose to believe — that we had some sort of a commitment — again, that was in your mind. Sheilah, we were both very young and new in this business. We both understood that it was going to be hard. Contrary to what everyone thinks, this is hard work, and you've got to know the profession inside and out. That's what I thought we were both doing out there. Neither of us was established. Neither of us — I thought — wanted commitments . . . and neither of us gave any, as I remember." His voice was crisp, angry.

"Not in words, no."

"That's what I deal in, Sheilah — words."
He crumpled his napkin and threw it on
the table. "Next time, sweetheart, ask about
commitments before you assume." He stood
up. "Come on, I think we're through with
this dinner."

"Maybe next time I should get commitments in writing."

He signaled the waiter and left money on
the table on top of the bill. "Not only in
writing, but sealed and notarized too." He
pulled her chair away from the table. "Let's
go."

They stood on the street corner, and she
stepped toward the curb.

"Don't bother to see me home, Simon.
I'll get a cab."

"I always see my women home." He took
hold of her elbow and propelled her toward
the parking lot and into his car. He put
on the radio, and they heard the announcer
give the news and time. Sheilah was startled
to realize it was after midnight.

"My!" she said sarcastically. "Cinderella's
gone to the ball with her Prince Charming
and missed the last pumpkin-coach ride
home. Now she's just wearing rags, and her
Prince Charming has reverted into just another big rat."

He double-parked the car in front of her apartment house. "Those clothes don't look like rags to me."

"You're right — they're not. I get lots of things at discount and secondhand! Including some of my dinner companions."

He touched his forehead. "Next time check out the price tag and quality of your merchandise, sweetheart. Some of it may be too expensive for even you."

She was still angry the next morning, and the small piles of neatly cut newspapers covering her desk not only perplexed but annoyed her.

"Where did this junk come from?" she demanded.

Beth poked her head into the office. "What junk?" She looked at the papers. "They're newspaper ads! Sale ads — for clothes, TV's, groceries — even hardware." She shrugged. "I don't know a thing about this. I spent the morning in the library and got here only a few minutes ago. Sorry." She picked up a sheet of white paper. "Here's a note," she said, and read aloud, " 'Your brand of merchandise?' "

Sheilah giggled. "He's crazy." And then, noticing Beth's still-puzzled expression, she put her hand to her lips, trying to stop the laughter. "Never mind, Beth. I think I know who did this."

"This all makes sense to you?"

"It sure does. I'll deal with it." She dialed a three-digit number.

"Yes." His voice was tired.

"It must have taken you a couple of hours to cut out all those ads."

"Until three o'clock in the morning to be exact. But that's okay, because I didn't have anything better to do with the night, thanks to you."

"I'm sorry about last night too. You know I have a terrible temper."

"That I remember."

"And I speak too quickly."

"Uh-huh."

"And sometimes I put my foot in my mouth."

"Yes, you do. It's a pretty foot, but you sure do abuse it."

"Come on, Simon, help make this easier for me. I'm also terrible about apologizing."

"Are you apologizing, Sheil?"

"Yes — for losing my temper, not for what I said."

"We'll discuss that another time."

"Maybe."

"Whatever you say, but I'll give you another chance for a fun time with Simon —

how about dinner tonight?"

"Thanks, but I can't."

"Some other time, then."

"Sure. Try me again. You might get lucky!" She winced at the flippant way the words came out.

"You're doing it again."

"I know — call it habit. Anyway, thanks." She hung up and leaned back against the chair, idly picking up the ads one by one, letting them slip through her fingers and flutter back onto the desk top. *Watch it, Sheilah,* she said to herself. *You're heading for trouble, and this time you're forewarned. This time you know what to expect!*

CHAPTER FIVE

She saw Simon come out of the audio booth with several scripts in his hand. "You're everywhere, aren't you?"

"Just checking something out with the engineers. There's a lot to learn when you move to another station."

"If you really need help, give me a call and I'll walk you through it. In two weeks you'll know everyone and everyplace in the station." She walked beside him. "We're really a friendly group — if you don't get in anyone's way. It's territorial, you know."

"Thanks for the offer, but Gretel's actually been helpful to me these past few days — she's shown me around, introduced me to some of the personnel. She's really making life smooth for me." He rustled the papers in his hand. "She's even helped me with a few angles I've been thinking about."

Sheilah smacked her lips together with a loud sucking noise. "That's our Gretel, all right. Always helpful, always friendly, and always after a man. If you're in Gretel's hands, then you're — and I emphasize *you're* — in good hands."

Simon fidgeted with the scripts, rolling them into neat cylinders. "You're being unkind to Gretel — she really has been helpful."

"I don't doubt that!"

"That's almost malicious, Sheilah," he said, turning down a hall and leaving her.

"Almost?" she yelled after him. "I must be slipping. I'll have to work on it." She passed the studios and stopped in front of a full-length mirror, automatically checking herself.

So, Gretel really was making a play for Simon, was she? Sheilah had a good notion to really give her a race for her money. She touched her hand to her head. *Sheilah Godfrey — are you mad?* she said to herself. *Do you realize what you're saying? It's nothing to you . . . none of your concern no matter what Gretel and Simon do. . . .* She looked once more at her reflection. *Besides, better her than me.*

The next day the weather turned wintry, and Simon shivered as he sat down beside Sheilah in the coffee shop.

"It's cold out there," he said, rubbing his hands together.

"Oh, no, certainly I don't mind, Simon. You can join me anytime," Sheilah said, moving her handbag.

He stood up quickly. "Hey, sorry, lady,

71

was this seat taken?"

"Stay — stay!" She patted his arm. "I'm just being extra-crazy today." She pointed outside to the street. "What do you mean cold? It's a great day. It's autumn . . . it's windy . . . it puts a healthy glow on your face. It's glorious." She turned back to him, her eyes sparkling.

"Oh, sure," he said. "I like windy days too. I especially like them when little bits of grit get into your mouth and you can crunch them with your teeth. Great for the dental caps! And it sure does put a chill on anything and everything."

"I told you this would be different. You made the move."

"You never give up, do you? Okay, so I like hot weather."

"Bad for your complexion."

He ignored her. "You can do more in the warm weather."

"I'll just bet you can," she mumbled into her cup.

He leaned on an elbow. "I'm curious. You say you love this weather, so tell me — what does one do around here when it's really cold?"

"Lots of things."

"Name them."

She pulled a small notebook from her briefcase. "You've just given me a great idea for a feature. Welcome to the city — this is what it's like in the winter." She wrote a few words on the lined paper. "Everything's always geared toward the tourist, but how about all the people who arrive in the city to live? They're out there, and they want to know what to do on a day-to-day, week-to-week basis. And especially on the weekends!" She looked up at him. "Good idea, huh?"

"Not bad, but you still haven't told me what you do in the winter."

"You bundle up, take long walks in the cold, window-shop, street-shop, people-watch in the park or on the street. You can eat hot chestnuts after they've warmed your hands, skate at Rockefeller Center, or just throw snowballs at trees, if you're inclined to. Lots of things."

"But they're all outdoor activities!"

"Of course they are. I thought you were a great outdoorsperson! But you could go to concerts, museums, visit friends — if you know any — sit in front of a fireplace, drink mulled wine, weekend at a ski lodge. . . ."

"Now that's sounding better and better to me."

"I should have known!" She looked at her watch. "Got to get going — I've got an appointment in twenty minutes, but I want to stop by Ben's office with this idea first."

"Hey!" he yelled at her across the shop. "You wouldn't like to do those last things with me, would you?" He leered at her, teasing her.

She widened her eyes and opened her mouth, simulating shock. "Why, Mr. Kent," she said in a mock Southern accent loud enough to attract the attention of the two men who sat at the coffee counter spreading cream cheese on their bagels, "what kind of woman do you take me for? I'm surprised you would even suggest something like that! If my daddy were here, you wouldn't take advantage of me. And he did so trust you!"

Simon choked on the last swallow of his coffee and saw that the two men hastily glanced at him and then turned back to eating their breakfast. When he looked at her through the glass window, she smiled and winked at him, and he raised his hand, made a fist, and shook it at her. She read his lips as he silently said, "I'll get you for this."

Ben okayed the feature as soon as Sheilah presented it.

"We're always getting calls from viewers about the weather and ski conditions and lodges, and I think it might be a good feature for the evening news," she said. "I can go and explore over a weekend and see just what's available in a two- or three-hour-drive radius."

"Why not?" Ben was enthusiastic. "Go on and do it as soon as possible — before it gets too late in the season. Do it this weekend if you want. Check with the weather bureau about what's coming up. They'll be able to give you an idea of the weather. I'll approve for you and the camera crew." Ben shuffled some papers on his desk, stood up, grabbed her hand, and began easing her out of the office. "Sorry, but I'm late for an appointment. Why don't you ask Simon to go along with you?"

"Why?"

"He's new to the area, and he might ask some good questions. And we can always use it as a promo for his show."

She wrinkled her nose. "That's not a good idea."

"Why not?"

"He might have other plans."

"So ask him anyway. Can't hurt." He hurried down the hall just as Simon turned a corner. "Here he is now — ask him."

"Ask me what?" Simon walked toward his office and she followed him inside.

"What are you doing this weekend?"

"Ah-ha!" He twirled an imaginary mustache. "You've decided to take me up on my invitation? You couldn't resist me!"

"Don't you wish! You know that idea I had about ski lodges in the area — to visit them and give a report to city dwellers about what to do in the winter?"

"Uh-huh." His voice was skeptical.

"Well, Ben thinks it would be a good idea for us — you and me — to go this weekend if the weather's okay. That is, if you've got no plans and are game for it."

Simon's eyes sparkled, and she tried not to remember the golden lights in his eyes that used to fascinate her.

"Sheilah love, you are asking me for a date."

"Sorry to disappoint you, but I'm doing it for the station. It was Ben's idea, not mine."

"And here I thought you wanted my body."

"No, love, it's only your TV body I crave." She picked up a proof of a publicity photo of him that was on his desk. "Nice, Simon, very nice, but I wonder how you'll look in a ski suit." She dropped the photo back onto the desk and eyed him critically. "Wait till your viewers see you coming down those slopes. Whoosh!" She got up and made a skiing motion as he leaned back in his chair, his hands clasped behind his neck.

"How good a skier are you?" he asked lazily.

"Fairly good. Not Olympic quality, but passable."

"Too bad! Not good enough."

She cocked her head. "Oh?"

"Did I ever tell you how I led my college team to the University World Skiing Championships?" He continued to lean back in his chair, and she took a step toward him.

"There's no such thing!"

He shrugged. "Are you sure?"

She hesitated. "No."

"Too bad," he repeated and then wheeled his chair around to face the window. "Three of the team members went on to the Olympics that next year. They did pretty well too — a silver and a bronze. The other fellow broke his ankle, though — that was a shame."

"You're impossible." She went through the open door of his office.

"Oh, and, Sheilah, ask the cameraman to photograph you from the side only in your ski suit — you've been eating enormous meals lately."

She heard his laugh as she pulled the door after her. This could be a bit difficult. He still did it — he could make her forget about all the bad times by simply saying something funny. She stood by the door, running her fingers up and down the cool pane of glass. What was it about him that was making her remember all those good times they'd had? She walked slowly to her own office. She thought she'd gotten completely over Simon. She thought she'd never let him into her life again. Now, she wondered.

CHAPTER SIX

It was exactly eleven-thirty by the clock on the TV set when Sheilah stepped forward and looked toward the back of the studio. "Okay, Simon, give me a minute and we can get going. Did I tell you Ben and Ginger are coming along too?"

"Yeah — it should be fun. Although," he said, grinning, "it might have been interesting with just the two of us."

She glared at him. "I told you this was a working weekend!"

"I know, I know." Simon held his hand up. "I was just kidding!"

A half hour later Simon drove his small sports car into the late-night weekend city traffic.

"I have to admit," he said, pulling into the left lane, "the city at night really gives me a good feeling. I like the idea of all these people having someplace to go and something to do. It doesn't make the city seem so cold."

"Simon's saying something nice?" Sheilah turned to face Ginger in the backseat. "Simon has never been a city boy. We used to call him the West Coast Adonis when I was out in California."

"You never told me that," Simon protested.

"I always saved my best lines about you for when you were out of earshot."

Ginger smiled and then yawned and put her head on Ben's shoulder. "Anybody mind if I go to sleep? It's not the company, honest. It's just that eight shows a week for the last six months have really exhausted me."

"We'll wake you when we get there." Ben tightened his arm around her shoulders. "Just as the show closed," he explained, "she got a call for another musical. She really needs this weekend." He shifted his body so that Ginger was more comfortable, and then he looked out the back window. "What was the weather forecast? I thought I heard something about an early snowfall."

"Uh-uh. I checked the long-range forecast this afternoon." Sheilah rubbed at the moisture on her window. "And they didn't mention any snow. It's supposed to be cold — twenties or low thirties — but nothing about precip." She turned to Simon. "I wasn't listening — they didn't change it, did they?"

"No, not really. A slight possibility of some snow in the mountains, that's all. Don't worry, if there's any threat, we'll get plenty of warning and just pack up early." He patted her arm. "Relax! This is going to be a fun weekend."

"Simon's right," Ben said. "Look at the night — there are stars in the sky. It's clear — nothing to worry about. When will the film crew get there?"

"Tomorrow. About noon. It'll give us time to scout around." She glanced out her side window at the deserted landscape. "It's absolutely beautiful out there, isn't it?"

Simon drove the car effortlessly through the countryside, and except for an occasional automobile that they passed coming toward them on the opposite side of the highway, the road was deserted, and their own headlights were the only lights to be seen for miles at a time.

"Pinetree Inn has been here since the 1800s. It used to be a resting place for travelers." Sheilah reached down to the folders in her handbag. "I've got to remember to include that in the tape."

"If I remember correctly," Simon said, "winter vacationers want their country inns old — preferably with some resident ghosts wandering around — but with all the modern conveniences too."

"I can guarantee you the old and the new, but I don't think there are any ghosts. At least none that I've heard about." She saw

81

the mischievous look on Simon's face. "Don't you dare, Simon. Don't you dare make up ghost stories for our viewers."

"They'd love it!"

"No!"

He shrugged and looked straight ahead at the road. She could see him in profile and noticed the way his hair had become disheveled when he shook his head. Her hands automatically moved toward him, wanting to reach out and smooth down the wayward lock, but she caught herself and stopped. To cover up the tentative gesture, she instead pulled her coat closer around her.

"Cold?" He reached for the heater knob.

"No. I was just making myself more comfortable." She took a deep breath. *Simon, please don't do too many nice things for me this weekend,* she thought. *There are times when I know I'm vulnerable.*

The steady pace of the car and the quiet, monotonous sound of the moving tires against blacktopped highways lulled her into drowsiness, and she only half heard Ben and Simon discussing the weekend. She snuggled farther down into her seat, pleasantly comfortable with the night, her companions, and herself. She tried to fight the overwhelming feeling of contentment that was overcoming her and making her drowsy, but the last thing she recalled was the way her body had half leaned toward Simon and the way her head just naturally rested on his shoulder. She smiled softly to herself and gave in to the sleep, not awaking until she felt a gentle nudging of her arm.

"We're here." Simon's voice was soft.

"Already?" She opened her eyes slowly.

"Already. It's magnificent."

She rubbed her eyes, looked through the windshield, and got her first glimpse of the inn, a three-story structure of dark brick and stone with several fireplace chimneys extending beyond the pitched roof. The first floor of the old building had several large floor-to-ceiling windows that were already partially shuttered against the cold fall air, and a wooden front door with a wrought-iron knocker in the center had thin slivers of frosted glass windows on the sides so that a distorted view of the lobby could be seen from the outside.

A large wooden porch surrounded the inn, and in one back section there were three or four wicker chairs that had not yet been stored away for the winter season.

There were two gas lampposts on either side of the wooden steps leading up to the porch, and in the moonlight the glow from the flickering swinging lamps cast eerie yet welcoming shadows on the front porch and on the evergreens surrounding the lodge. The soft scraping of iron against iron gave testimony to the fact that a windy cold front was starting to move in.

"Well, what do you think?" Ben had already gotten out of the car and had two suitcases in his hands. "This what you wanted for the first show?"

"Exactly!"

"It's probably something you conjured up just to make all new East Coast residents welcome." Simon looked around. "Imagine having something so peaceful so close to the city!"

They went through the unlocked door and into the huge lobby, which was furnished in pine and oak and flowered chintz. There were several deep, cushioned couches positioned around the room, and off to one side there was a huge stone fireplace, its fire slowly dying.

"Evening. You folks the TV people?" The gray-haired man behind the oak desk leaned on his elbows.

"That's right." Simon approached the desk.

"I know. I recognize you from television. You're Simon, aren't you — from 'Simon Says'?"

Simon nodded.

"Are you hungry? We thought you might be after that long drive, so we kept something on the stove in the kitchen just in case." The older man indicated another room next to the lobby. "If you want, you all can check into your rooms while we set the table. It's nothing fancy, but it might taste good if you're hungry."

"We're starved!" Sheilah walked to the desk, picked up a pen, and signed her name in a big maroon book.

"Room 108 — on the second floor, at the top of the stairs." He offered the pen to Simon. "My name's Lawrence Edward, and my wife, Irene, and I own Pinetree Inn. Actually, it's been in her family since it was built, but none of her brothers wanted to take care of the place — we were the only ones interested in keeping it up. So we come by it by default, actually. Still, we like it, and we hope you will too."

He turned the book around so that he could read the signatures.

"Mr. Kent, you'll be in 106, right next to Ms. Godfrey. There's a connecting door that can be opened" — he looked up at Sheilah — "or you can bolt it anytime you like." He handed them large, wrought-iron keys. "If you go out, you can either carry the key with you or leave it at the desk.

There's a doorbell and a door knocker if you're out late and the place is locked up. We'll hear either one and let you in." He turned back to register Ben and Ginger.

Sheilah picked up her bag and moved quickly up the carpeted staircase, down a short hall, and to the door of her room. She stepped into a medium-sized bedroom that smelled of polished lemon and lavender. She took a deep breath. The last time she'd smelled something like this she was all of about eight years old and had visited Great-aunt Jeannette in her big old Victorian house. She put her bag down gently on the round, braided rug in the middle of the room. She sniffed hard, inhaling the aroma of the room, and sat down on the soft bed, resting her head against the feather pillow underneath the green-and-pink quilt. One shoe fell onto the floor, and she started to kick the other off just as Simon came through the open door.

"Oh no, you don't! You're hungry and you've got to get something to eat."

"I'd rather go to sleep."

"Uh-uh! The Edwards are probably fixing something for you right now."

"Simon, have pity on me — I'm exhausted."

"No way. I remember you used to go

without food when you were on one of your ridiculous diets and then you'd come to work with a headache. You need to eat something."

"We've all been up since early this morning. I'm too tired to eat."

He reached out and tugged at her arm. "Come on."

She forced her foot into her shoe. "Still bossing people, I see." She looked back once more at the soft, warm bed.

"Come on, I promise you can go back to sleep after you eat — in fact, I'll even tuck you in."

She jumped up. "Forget it! And don't get any funny ideas. This weekend is strictly business. Remember?"

He started to laugh. "At least I got you up."

Mr. Edward was putting some hot biscuits and butter on the bare, polished-pine round table when they entered the dining room.

"Mrs. Edward made these this evening, and we put them aside for you," he said, lifting ceramic covers from dishes as Sheilah and Simon sat down in two ladder-back chairs that were pulled up to the table. "Just some scrambled eggs with sharp cheese, but you'll like them," the innkeeper said as the aroma of the hot biscuits and butter mingled with the cheddar scent. "The coffee's perking and will be ready in a minute, and there's some fresh applesauce in this bowl." He watched both of them reach for the biscuits. "I'll get the coffee."

Sheilah took a forkful of eggs. "You're right, I was hungry."

"I see you still do it."

"What?"

"Talk with your mouth full."

"I —"

"I have a lot to say." They spoke in unison.

"You always used to say that too," Simon said.

"Simon, do me a favor, don't do that this weekend."

"Do what?"

"Remember."

He broke off a bit of the biscuit and slowly buttered it. "Why not?"

"For a couple of reasons. One, we're here to do a job. And two, I don't think I want to remember anything that you and I did or didn't do before." She watched as he ate the biscuit. "As far as I'm concerned we're here to tape. And if we have fun along the way . . . so be it." She speared some of the eggs onto her fork. "Agreed?"

"Agreed, but —" He looked up at her briefly and then down again at the butter. "Somewhere along the line, whether it's here or in New York, you're going to have to deal with the fact that once upon a time we did have a whale of a time together. It happened, and we can't change that, Sheilah."

She nodded and continued eating slowly and in silence. Finally Mr. Edward took the last of the plates away. "Well, if you two don't want anything else, I'll just clear away everything and close up. I'll leave the coffeepot here, though, if you'd like — it's got another couple of cups in it and you two can sit awhile by the fire. Not much of a blaze, but there's still a lot of warmth from it." He started up the stairs. "I'll say good night to you folks."

"Want to have one more cup?" Simon shook the coffeepot. "There's actually enough for a half more."

"No, you take it." Sheilah stood near the fire, watching the little sparks shoot out from the dying embers. Simon joined her, standing close to her so that she could see out of the corner of her eye the way his fingers wrapped around the coffee mug.

"I think the best part of a fire is these last few moments," he said. "There's something peaceful about them."

"I know. When I was a little girl, I used to like it when the logs were piled high and there would be a huge blaze. But then I realized that that only represented some sort of flash fire — that it was over in a few minutes, and then what?"

"Like life." He motioned toward the fireplace. "Sometimes you get caught up in the brightness and the roar of it and you want to be part of that blaze, and then somewhere along the way you just get tired of all the sparks, and that's when you — at least, that's when I — come to appreciate a quiet, steady glow."

"It's contentment."

"That's it." He sat down in one of the big couches. "Didn't you ever just want to sit and watch the flames?"

She stared at the small flecks of fire. "You're looking at the original flame-watcher. I can tell you just about the entire life cycle of a fire." She leaned closer to the fireplace so that the golden highlights in her hair glistened and her skin became dewy. "We're down to the last faint glimmers now. It'll take another hour or so, but the fire's just about out." She picked up a long metal fire tong and poked at the bits of charred wood lying on the stone floor of the fireplace, causing sparks to burst and sputter. "See?" she said. "The fire is really over."

"Like us?" She barely heard his words as she laid the tongs down on the hearth, yet she nodded. Then she raised her hands to her cheeks and slowly turned to face him.

"Are you sorry?" he asked, and when she didn't reply, he added, "Sometimes I am. These last couple of weeks with you, at the studio, have made me realize —" He put his cup down on the table and started to stand, but she shook her head and he paused, so that she was able to stop momentarily what she knew she almost wanted to happen.

"It's late," she said, glad for the excuse of the heat of the fire as the cause of her burning cheeks.

He moved closer to her and very softly touched her hand, letting his fingers play gently on the pulse in her wrist.

"No," she said, and when she didn't move her hand, he tightened his grip around it, pulling her closer to him.

"No," she repeated, still not moving her hand. "We said good-bye once."

"We never said good-bye," he answered as his hand moved slowly along her sweatered arm, past the bend in her elbow, past her forearm and her shoulder, and finally stopped on her neck, all the time pulling her closer to him. "You left a note. We never said good-bye." He whispered the words into her hair.

She closed her eyes and pressed her forehead into his shoulder, smelling his shaving scent, and she remembered vividly all the times he had held her. And as his arms moved to enfold her completely, she raised her head so that she was able to receive his kiss.

"Everything's changed, and yet nothing has changed," he whispered, kissing her again.

"No! You're only half right," she said, suddenly realizing what was happening. She moved away from him. "Everything's changed, Simon. We're five years past."

He reached out for her once more, but she stepped back. "No, Simon, this isn't California. It's too late for us."

He smiled, and she recognized the ruefulness of it from the few times he'd had to acknowledge that he couldn't have his way.

"Is it really?"

"Yes. Good night, Simon," she said softly. A few minutes later she heard his footsteps pause at her door, then continue past to his room.

She lay awake watching the moon through her window. *Simon, oh, Simon! We've come a long way. Everything's changed. We're not the same people. Just because I loved you once doesn't mean I can love you again. Too much has happened to us. Let's just be friends, Simon . . . let's just be friends.* She tossed on the bed.

CHAPTER SEVEN

The rapping at the door was loud and Simon's voice was insistent. "Time to get up, Sheilah."

"Go away. I'm sleeping." She pulled the warm blanket over her head.

He knocked again. "Then wake up. You've got a problem."

She kicked the blanket off, reached for her robe and tied it around her. "This had better be for real, Simon," she said as she opened the door, "or else *you've* got a problem."

"It's for real, all right," he said, grinning at her. "Snow."

"Snow?"

"As in snowstorm. As in today. As in by noon."

"You're joking?"

He shook his head.

"You're not joking!" She pulled at a lock of hair, curling it around her finger. "It wasn't supposed to — they said 'maybe,' and then only a few flakes." She looked toward the shuttered windows. "Have you told Ben?"

"Yeah. He and Ginger are delighted. He

said he hopes it snows for forty days and forty nights."

"He would. He's been saying they needed some time together."

"They're going to get it."

"No chance the storm will bypass us?"

Simon shook his head. "I called the station and asked for the latest weather readout, and they confirmed it. Said it was a freak early storm."

"Okay, give me about fifteen minutes to get dressed, and I'll meet you downstairs."

"Listen, if you'd prefer to stay in your room. . . ." He gave her a playful leer.

"Get serious, will you? It's a wonder they don't call your show 'Simple Simon.' "

"Clever . . . clever, Sheilah."

"Go. I'll see you in a few minutes."

It was closer to a half hour when she got to the breakfast table where Simon was already seated.

"So? Any ideas?" She sipped her juice.

"Uh-huh. As I see it, we have two choices. We can go home now before the storm hits, or we can stay and shoot tape while the snow comes down. If we go home, we'll miss the camera crew that's probably already on its way here, and we'll have no footage. But if we stay, at least we'll get some tape in the can. We're not due back at the station until Monday anyway — two whole days from now."

"That's what I was thinking. What does Ben say? Never mind — he's still hoping for a repeat of the forty days' flood." She broke off a piece of one of the blueberry muffins in a deep dish next to Simon's breakfast plate. "What about you — you have a say in this."

"I'm game. I've got nothing better to do. Besides, it's one of the hazards of the job."

"Thanks."

"You know what I mean." He slowly buttered the remaining piece of muffin and handed it to her.

"Actually," she said, "it could work out well. We wanted to show the kinds of recreation available in the area on a typical winter weekend. This is it. We'll tape walking in the woods, hiking, looking at the scenery — we'll explain the countryside. This evening we can sit around the fire, toast marshmallows, talk to some other guests, play a couple of games — show the relaxing side of the vacation." She looked past him toward a window.

"Isn't that what a lot of people want — just to relax?"

"That, and skiing. But we'll ski tomorrow." She refilled their coffee cups. "If you were a stranger to the area, what would you want to do?"

"What more could a man want? Fresh air, excitement, good times, and a beautiful woman. I feel like a stranger in paradise."

"You're putting it on a bit thick, aren't you? I guess, though, you've got to add some new wrinkles to your stock phrases — to go along with those on your face."

Simon touched his cheeks. "Still hollows there."

"But they're beginning to fill in, love." She took out her notes. "Let me make a phone call and see when the crew will get here."

She returned in a few minutes and sat on the window seat in the lobby.

"It's going to be a blizzard! I really thought I had all bases covered, but *this!*"

"Act of God!" Ben and Ginger were beside her. "We don't mind."

"I didn't think you would." Sheilah shifted and turned to look at Simon, who was standing by the fireplace. "Well, how about it? Want to scout locations with me? The crew will be here in a couple of hours."

"I've been looking forward to it."

"Simon, you're lying. If anyone had told me two months ago that you'd be here, telling me that you want to go walk in the snow,

I would have bet them a week's salary."

"You two love to needle each other, don't you?" Ginger said.

"I'll explain it to you later," Ben said quietly.

"No, I think I understand it perfectly."

"Nothing to understand, Ginger, we're just friends." Sheilah pulled a blue knit cap down over her hair. "Let's go, Simon."

The snow was falling rapidly, and the tiny flakes had already started to conceal the dirt walks and winter-dried grass that led away from the inn. There were small piles of snow at the base of the surrounding trees, and their bare branches, already dusted with white, appeared to be wrapped in heavy thicknesses of cotton batting.

There was a grayness to the outside as a result of the heavy, snow-laden clouds that hovered and seemed to cover the entire area, and the only sound that seemed to penetrate was the soft, almost no-sound of the steadily falling snow. Only an occasional muffled thud was heard as small, snow-heavy branches broke and fell to the ground, leaving long imprints on the white drifts beneath the trees.

A cold gust of wind picked up and whirled and eddied in front of them, and they both shivered involuntarily, hunching their shoulders and bending their heads to deflect the brunt of the biting snow.

"You really like this stuff?" Simon asked as he wiped away at the flakes landing on his face. "You honest to goodness *like* this weather? All this white stuff sticking on you?"

"It makes you come alive."

"Sure, if it doesn't kill you first." He clapped his hands together. "How about that barn and those trails over there for color?"

"Good. When people think of going to a ski lodge, they want to know what makes it cozy and inviting and fun. They don't want to ski twenty-four hours a day. Showing the barn — that sets the mood." She blew into the cold air and saw her breath deflect the tiny snowflakes in front of her.

"Oh, really?" He grabbed her shoulders and turned her toward him so that her face was close to his and her scarf brushed against his parka. "It's nice to know you learned something from me."

"What?" He was standing close to her, his hands on her shoulders, and she blinked, trying to concentrate on what he was saying.

"My Sunday-afternoon show — in California — the one that had a segment on sight-seeing," he reminded her.

It was the way he smiled when he teased her that she remembered from before, and she brushed at her eyes as if to clear them.

"I'd completely forgotten."

"Selective amnesia, I call it."

"No, really, I hadn't thought about that for years."

"Have you thought anything about me these past years?"

"No, not at all. I was much too busy to think about you."

"I doubt that, lady. There was a time when you remembered everything about me."

She dug the toes of her boots into the snow and then bent down and scooped up a handful of it and threw it at him. "There was a time when I wanted to."

"But not now?" He lobbed a small snowball at her, and she ducked.

"Lousy shot. No, I find you quite forgettable now, thank you." She grinned and pointed to the left. "Let's check out the territory for color. We might want to shoot it later."

He kicked at the snow. "Careful, this is treacherous stuff — there's ice below the snow."

He reached out to take her arm as her foot slid, and she clung to him. "Give me your hand," he ordered. Her foot slipped again, and she held tightly to him, taking small steps until she was on firmer ground. "We're going to be lucky to get out of here tomorrow night if this keeps up. I thought you said snow doesn't arrive in these parts until the end of the month."

"It's a wonderland." She stood beneath a large pine tree. "Look around you — only a Scrooge couldn't see the beauty of this." She waved her hand, taking in the entire landscape. "In another couple of hours this is going to look like a Christmas card." She brushed snow off her eyelashes, and she saw him look at her with a softness in his eyes.

"You look like something out of a Christmas card."

"A ghost of Christmas past?"

He turned his head so that his voice was muffled by the wind, and she barely heard him. "Why don't you let it alone, Sheilah?" But before she had a chance to answer, he pointed to another location. "That stand of trees might be a better camera angle." He walked ahead of her toward the snow-frosted pines.

I can't let it alone, Simon, she thought. *I have to keep reminding myself of who we are and who we once were. Because this is the way it has to be — or else . . . or else, Simon, it would be so easy to fall in love with you again. . . .*

He stopped at the trees. "This spot's got

more going for it — more branches, and there's a great space here where it looks like you're nestled within the tree itself." She watched as he pushed back the feathery pine needles, oblivious to the snow that he was shaking down onto his head and shoulders. She reached out to brush the heavy dusting from his ski jacket. Her touch startled him, and as her hand swept over his shoulders he turned and stared at her, his face first tightening then relaxing as he realized what she was doing.

"The snow — it was falling on you." She slapped her gloved hands. "Look, Simon, we made a deal, remember? And if there are things that remind us of other days — and there will be, I admit — let's just ignore them. And," she added, seeing him half smile, "let's change the subject." She tossed her head back so that her face was exposed to the sky and the full blast of cold air settled on her cheeks. A snowflake fell onto her face close to the corner of her mouth, and she flicked her tongue at the spot and felt the icy liquid drop.

Simon took hold of her arm again. "Don't, Sheilah," he said deliberately, "don't try to erase all the memories. It's part of life — part of our lives." He touched her face where the melted flake had been. "I know what you're doing, what you're feeling. I'm feeling it too."

"No, no, you don't. We're not feeling anything. It's only the setting — the timing — it's really only an illusion." She pushed his hand away.

"Okay, this time you win," he said and then looked up at the sky, which was darkening rapidly. "Come on, let's get back to the inn and get the crew before it snows harder. I think we'd better get our shots in the can as soon as possible, because I don't think we'll be wanting to shoot later."

They worked all afternoon, filming the scenes they wanted to use for their first show, and by the time they took a break the snow was falling faster and heavier and the sky had turned a deep charcoal-gray.

"According to the farmers that dark sky means it's going to continue snowing for at least another twelve hours," Mark, the director, said.

Sheilah wiped at her cold-burning eyes. "I think we've got enough outdoor film for today. We've got some good shots. All we need now are a few more random scenes with a focus on the falling snow, and that should wrap it up. We'll get some footage tonight, by the fire — maybe a few feet of the snow at night . . . art stuff — and then tomorrow we'll do the skiing down the trails. They tell me there's a killer slope nearby." She looked over at Simon, who was helping the crew. "That's more your style! I think they call it Devil's Pass!"

"Still don't think I can ski, huh?" He grinned. "Wait until tomorrow."

She picked up her cue sheets and began to follow the crew as it headed for the inn. "Gladly. Right now I'm freezing, and my feet have turned to two blocks of ice. Let's go."

The snow had already obliterated the bottom step. As they finally walked up onto the porch Simon turned and looked once more at the white-blanketed grounds surrounding the lodge.

"You're right, it is a beautiful sight."

"Right now I can't look at any more snow. All I want to do is get these boots off and get warm." She sat on a pine bench in a small alcove off the lobby and began peeling off her ice-encrusted gloves, but when she bent down to unzip her wet boots, her numbed fingers kept slipping against the metal.

"Here, let me. You look exhausted." He bent down in front of her and placed her foot onto his knee, carefully pulling down the zipper. "Now the other one," he said as she took her foot out of the cold boot.

"They really are numb." She reached down, but Simon had already begun to massage her stockinged feet, rubbing them so that at last she began to wriggle her toes. "I owe you one, Simon. Remind me someday. But right now I'm going upstairs to get out of these wet things. Thanks for your help."

She had already changed into her robe and was toweling her hair when she heard a knock on the door, and when she answered it, Simon thrust a cup of steaming dark tea toward her. "Drink this, then take a hot bath, and you'll feel better."

"That's two I owe you."

"I thought you said you knew how to take care of yourself." He shook his head. "Go on," he said, pulling the door closed as he left, "go take your bath."

She had intended to sit on the bed for just a few moments, but the quick contrast of the cold outside air and the warmth of the room had put her to sleep, and when she awoke, it was dark. She stared into the black room and then realized that she was lying on her bed and that a blanket had been thrown over her. She rubbed her eyes just as she heard a click, and she turned toward the door as a shaft of light streaked her room and fell across the foot of her bed.

Simon was standing in the doorway.

"Well, you've finally gotten up." He pointed to the adjoining door. "You left it unlocked." He walked into her room. "Don't worry, I didn't make a pass at you."

"You're darn right you didn't make a pass at me," she said, suddenly alert. "A lot of good it would do you, anyhow."

" 'Thanks for taking care of me, Simon,' " he said, mocking her. "Now why did I think that that would be the correct response?"

"Response? What were you doing in my room?"

" 'Gee, thanks, Simon, for seeing if I was all right.' " He brushed back his hair. "You didn't come down for a couple of hours and we were all waiting for you, so I came up to see if you were okay. When you didn't answer, I went into my room and then I tried the door. It opened, and there you were — fast asleep and the teacup about to fall off the bed. I took it away, got the blanket out of the closet, covered you, and went downstairs. 'Gee, thanks, Simon, for taking care of me,' " he said again. "And besides, I've never been accused of making a pass at a sleeping beauty in my life."

"Oh, really? I just assumed that all —"

"You always assumed too much, lady. Or," he added, squinting his eyes at her, "maybe you hoped for too much."

"My days of hoping for you ended a long time ago."

"So you've said over and over and over again." He grinned and she shrugged, and he motioned toward the edge of the bed. "Now that that scene has been played, mind if I sit down?"

She laughed. "Oh, sure, here." She moved her legs under the warm blanket so that he could sit beside her.

"I really just wanted to see if you were okay, that's all." He patted her hand. "Look, you've told me in so many ways that I'm to keep my distance, and I will."

He shook his head and she could see in the light that had filtered from the doorway that there was a perplexed look on his face. "But, Sheilah, once upon a time we were more than friends, and you can't deny that. Nor can we pretend that we've only just met. I wish — really wish, Sheilah — that we could be friends . . . and maybe something even more if it happens. But you've put up such a barrier. . . ." His voice trailed off. "Anyway, if you want dinner, it's in ten minutes." He closed the door, and the room went dark again.

She slowly dressed. Why was this happening again? How could he just come back into her life like this? And why was she letting him?

CHAPTER EIGHT

Ginger stretched lazily and kissed Ben's cheek. "Want to take a walk? It's so romantic out there. . . ."

"Sounds good to me too," Simon said.

"Oh?" Ginger silently questioned Sheilah.

"Forget it, Ginger," she said. "Simon and I have known each other too well and too long for there to be anything romantic between us. We're strictly friends." She grabbed Simon's hand and led him to the door.

"Sure. Anything you say." Ginger seemed unconvinced. "We'll meet you outside."

"You should really speak for yourself." Simon adjusted his scarf against the first blast of cold air.

"About what?" Sheilah pulled on her hat.

"That crack about knowing me too well and too long to be involved romantically."

"It's true!" They walked down the porch steps.

"Are you sure?"

"Positive. I know that right now we're going through the 'remembrances of things past' routine, but that's all we're feeling. You're a romantic person — I am too —

but it would never work again, Simon, so let's not waste our time."

"Afraid?" Again that one-sided grin she remembered.

"Of you? Not on your life. I've recovered from you. My heart's in fine shape now. It doesn't even skip a beat when I see you in the hall."

"Did it ever?"

"A few years ago, yes. Now, no way!" She leaned against the side of the barn and looked around her. Small snowflakes were continuing to fall, and even though there was a cloud-hidden moon, the entire landscape glowed a brilliant sparkling white that seemed to immobilize and freeze the scene as though it had been painted on a canvas. The only intrusion on the pristine setting was the dark curls of smoke that were spiraling out and upward from the lodge chimneys, their pungent fumes intermingling with the crisp clear air and falling snowflakes so that they perfumed the entire area with the odor of burning pine and applewood.

Simon watched her. "Tell me what you're thinking. You look so content."

"I am. I was just wondering what the rest of the world is doing tonight. This is so beautiful. I can't think of anywhere I'd rather be right now." She brushed at a flake.

"Things like that. How about you? Are you wishing that it were warm and sunny and that you were a million miles away from all this?" She blew into the cold air so that she could see her breath vaporize in front of her.

"No."

"No? You surprise me."

"Why? I'm not the same person you knew in California. You're not either. We're both different now."

They walked slowly on the path leading to where the gardens would normally be but which were now marked only by clumps of snow-adorned bushes that flanked the completely covered walkways.

"Am I?" She swept her hand across the top of a bush, scattering the snow so that it sparkled as it fell to the ground.

"Yes. Much." He took a deep breath and looked out toward the trees, and for a moment she thought she saw his eyes half close in thought. Then he shook himself gently and looked at her. "Sorry, I sometimes get lost too."

"Tell me how I've changed."

"They're only my opinions. They're personal. But that's the only way I can compare them to before."

"Still, tell me. I'm interested."

He hesitated. "Okay. Well, for one thing you're softer." He said it quietly, factually.

"Softer! That's a terrible word to use about me."

"Why? Where is it written that you can't be professional and soft?"

"You'll spoil my image." She wrinkled her nose.

"Stop clowning, Sheilah, and let me talk. You can have your say later." He waited a second and then continued, "Good, you're listening. That's one of the changes. You never gave me a chance to talk."

"You never wanted to."

"That's because you were always so busy trying to one-up me. That's part of what I'm talking about. And you're still doing it, by the way. What I'm talking about is that you're more at peace with yourself. Probably because you're happy with who you are and with the job you're doing. It's — it's" — he waved his hand in the air, swirling the snowflakes high above their heads so that they fell in a tumbling, continuous turning until they landed on the ground — "more like you've learned from life . . . that you realize it's not so bad, so harsh out there. It's like you're —" He looked up and began to laugh. "Can you believe it, Sheilah, all I can think of is that you're softer. How's that for an ad-lib?" He swirled his foot in the snow. "An anchorman — an on-his-feet interviewer — and all I can say is that you're softer." He laughed again, and this time she nodded her head.

"Anything else?"

"Oh, there's a lot more. Want me to continue?"

"Sure! You're doing fine."

"Well, this is like when I first met you, but it isn't. You laugh a lot more now. As though — as though you're in love. Are you?"

"No." *At least I don't think I am,* she amended silently. *I'd better not be. Not again, Simon . . . not with you.*

"Were you — I mean, after we split?"

"I thought I was, but I wasn't. Just a reaction, I think. I will admit, Simon, you were a tough act for anyone to follow."

"So were you."

"Thanks. Were you — in love with anyone?" She asked it tentatively, almost shyly.

He shook his head vigorously so that flakes on his hair fell pinwheel style to the sides. "No. Like you, I thought I was. About five or six times, to tell you the truth. But they never were what I'd consider 'real.' Somehow they never worked out."

"That's how I felt. Like something was missing."

"Yeah. And something was."

Don't say anything more, Simon, she thought. *Please.*

"I don't think you were searching for the same thing I was by the third or fourth romance," Simon continued. He blew into the air so that the flakes scattered. "I was looking for something I realized I once had but lost." She could barely hear his words. "Look, let's not continue this anymore," he said abruptly. "You don't want to hear this. Maybe it's just the setting, like you said."

Oh, Simon, don't say things like this to me. Don't confess to me. Don't make me want you again. She cleared her throat. "You're right, remembrances of things past can do strange things to you."

They walked past ice-and-snow-encapsulated thorny rose branches that had not been pruned back in the fall and that now reached out and swayed in the wind. One especially long crystal-like branch scraped her cheek as she passed, leaving a small welt across her face, and she involuntarily cried out at the suddenness of the scratch.

Simon stopped and looked at the redness on her cheek. "Does it hurt?"

"No. I just wasn't expecting it, that's all."

He brushed her cheek with his bare finger. "I don't think there are any splinters." He peered closely at her cheek, his head bending near hers so that she smelled the lingering scent of the inn's wood fire on his clothes.

"It's all right, really. Besides, a lot of people say I have thick skin."

"Quit the act, Sheilah," he said gruffly as he continued to gently wipe the welt.

Oh, Simon! she thought. *We're much too close to the edge now. If only this were five years ago, I would hold you forever and ever. If only . . . if only. Once upon a time I loved you, Simon. I really loved you.*

A snowflake fell close to the outer corner of her eye, melting almost immediately as it touched her skin. The small droplet moved slowly toward the welt. Simon looked at it and then into her eyes as though he could read her mind. Her throat tightened and she was afraid to speak — afraid that no sound would emerge and that the absence of it would betray her.

Slowly his hand moved from the red mark on her cheek to the corner of her eye, smudging the moisture with his finger, slowly tracing its path as it fell away from her cheek into and beyond her woolen cap, so that his finger mingled with her hair and the rest of his hand lay lightly on the side of her face.

She took a deep breath just as his lips

came down, first gently, and then roughly, on hers. She closed her eyes and gave in to the emotions his kiss aroused in her. She reached up and pulled him closer, and his hold tightened on her as they clung to each other and continued the kiss. She imagined herself swirling, much like the snowflakes, round and round until the breath inside her felt as though it would puncture her lungs.

"I —"

"Don't say anything," he whispered. "Don't say a word. Later. . . ." His lips lingered at the corner of her mouth before he moved them over hers again.

Somewhere in the distance she heard the soft thud of a falling branch, and they raised their heads, both taking deep breaths of the icy air in rapid and almost identical rhythms.

"Sheilah, I —"

She stepped back. "No, don't say anything, Simon. I'm going back."

"Sheilah, wait!" He put his hand on her arm.

"What for?" She shook her head. "Let's just forget this."

"I think we've got to at least talk about what happened."

"No. Let's just say it was the place and the time that made it happen. We were just caught up in it. Sometimes it's best to just forget, Simon."

"Is that what you really think we should do? Forget what just happened?" he yelled at her retreating back. "You won't forget it so easily, Sheilah. You can't."

She turned and stood there, her hands clenched at her sides. "I have to!" she yelled at him so that she heard an echo of her own words through the trees. "I don't want to love you again, Simon. Don't you understand? I don't want to love you again." She put her cold mittens to her face and spoke into them, muffling her words. "And I'm afraid I do."

CHAPTER NINE

When Sheilah awoke the next morning she remembered falling asleep thinking about Simon, thinking that she didn't want him in her life again, that she wanted to forget the scene in the snow. *It was only the setting,* she kept repeating until she fell asleep. *Only the setting.*

Today would be different, she told herself. *I won't be alone with him. I won't give him the chance to — I won't give myself a chance to —* She grabbed her parka. *Oh, Simon, why did you come back into my life?*

She saw Ben in the dining room. "Where is everyone?"

"If you mean by everyone, where are Simon and Mark — they're outside shooting footage on the slopes."

"Why didn't you call me?" She looked at the large grandfather's clock. "It's only ten o'clock."

"Simon said he knocked on your door, but when you didn't answer he thought he would help you out and let you sleep late."

"Simon said *what?* Ben, this is my show. What gets into everyone? As soon as Simon

117

comes on the scene, everyone begins to take it for granted that he speaks for me. That was a big part of the problem in California, everyone just assuming that Simon and I — Oh, never mind."

"I'm sorry, Sheilah. "I just naturally thought —"

"You just proved my point, Ben. You just 'naturally thought.' What is it with Simon that makes everyone see his point of view? Sometimes I think I hate the day that he came aboard." She drank her coffee. "I'm going out to see if the crew needs me."

"We already shot most of it." Ben's voice was hesitant. "Simon and Mark directed, and we —"

"Oh, swell. Now he's taking over my job." She nodded her head. "First my life, then my job. And you, Ben, you're the one who knows me so well and you just go along with all this." She turned toward the door as Simon and Mark came through it. "Never mind. Here comes Mr. Wonderful now."

Simon smiled at her. "Wait till you get out there, Sheilah. You're going to love it."

She glared at him. "Simon, you're stepping onto my territory. This is my show. Remember?"

His smile faded. "Hey, I thought you'd be surprised — and pleased."

118

"I'm not. And I'm not happy that you three went out without me. Stop taking things — and me — for granted. I warned you before."

Ben saw the storm brewing and quietly took his leave.

"Wait a minute," Simon said, moving closer to Sheilah. "I'm not taking you — I thought I'd help you out."

"Don't patronize me, Simon. I'm a big girl and can take care of myself and my productions."

"Whoa." He put up his hand. "Back off. So I made a mistake — hey, I'm sorry."

"You've been making a lot of mistakes this weekend."

"Ah, then this really has nothing to do with my shooting footage for you. It's about yesterday, isn't it?"

She looked down at the floor and then up at him, her eyes blazing. "You come into my life and try to take up where you left off — take over my job, take over me. This isn't California, Simon. You had your chance there, and you blew it. Now stay out of my life and stay out of my job."

"I — okay, I will. I'm sorry if I upset you. But hey," he said, seeing that the others in the room were avoiding looking at them, "let's continue our private argument some other time."

"There won't be another time. Not for anything."

"Okay." Simon's voice was quiet. "If that's what you really want."

"I do."

"Fine, but let's not jeopardize the show. You really do have some good footage there. Take a look at it. If you don't like it, then you can scrap it and shoot some other film. But at least look at it."

"Of course I'll look at it. But next time, let me do my own job, okay?"

"Sometimes I just don't understand you. You're the one who asked me along this weekend. You're the one who wanted my opinions. I thought we worked well together."

"First off, bringing you along wasn't my idea, it was Ben's. And second, what you did wasn't helping out. What you did was take over my job. That's exactly what I worried about when you said you were accepting the job at our station."

"Hey, lighten up." Simon's voice was low. "It's no big deal. It never was in the old days. We always helped each other out. Remember?"

"Enough, Simon. Stop talking about the old days. You really think this is like the old days? It's not. This is my turf, not yours."

She caught her breath. "I didn't mean that."

"I think you meant exactly what you said. Sorry, Sheilah, it won't happen again. Nothing will happen again." He walked stiffly out of the room.

Ginger and Ben were watching her. "I blew it, didn't I?" she asked them.

Ginger nodded. "It sure looks that way."

"I shouldn't have lost my temper, but he makes me so darn angry." She put on her parka. "Forget it. I'll be back in a little while." She closed the door behind her.

"I wouldn't be so harsh on yourself if I were you." She heard Simon's voice behind her as she stood by the pine tree where they had first shot film.

"How'd you find me?"

"I remembered how you were when we were in California — how I'd find you at a favorite place after we'd had one of our old shouting matches." He looked around. "We've come a long way from the sunny beaches." He put out a snowy glove to her. "Hey, I'm really sorry."

"No. I'm ashamed of my outburst. I try to keep things under control, but I guess I try too hard sometimes. It's my old defenses getting the better of me." She reached out to his hand. "Let's both just chalk it up to the weather."

"Deal. Want to go back to the inn now?"

"Not yet. I just want the quiet for a few more minutes."

"Want company?"

"Not really. I don't feel like talking. I want to work some things out in my mind." She touched an ice-crusted branch.

"I'll stay, but I promise I won't say a word." He stood by the tree, watching as small icicles fell from the pine needles as she ran her hand over the smooth ice.

"Simon, you're right. I can't avoid certain things. We were very close once. We still have some attraction for each other. And we still enjoy each other. So instead of denying it, why don't we just acknowledge all these things?"

"Right."

"And now," she said, looking at him very carefully, "now that I've acknowledged all this, what do I do about it?"

"Want my suggestion?" He leaned against a snowy pine trunk.

"Go ahead — you're involved."

"Let's just see where it takes us."

"That's probably what I'm afraid of —" She snapped an icicle in half. "That got us into trouble last time, and, truthfully, I don't want to go through all that pain again."

"So what's your solution?"

"I don't have any."

"Then as long as you don't have one, why not follow mine? I promise not to rush you, push you, or get in your way."

"It wouldn't work. We've been through too much to trust each other."

"Would I lie to you?"

"Yes."

"Not this time, sweetheart," he said, mimicking Humphrey Bogart.

"It's still a lousy imitation." She kicked at the snow and shoved her hands into her pockets. "Come on, we've got to get a move on — we have to leave."

Ginger and Ben met Sheilah in the lobby.

"It's been a lovely weekend." Ginger looked fondly at Ben. "I'm sorry to end it. Next week this time, let's see, I'll be in Philadelphia in tryouts." She danced a few steps. "Not too rusty for a long weekend layover, am I?"

"Okay, Sheilah," Simon said, coming down the steps, "let's get the car on the road! Fun time's over." He headed for the door with his own overnight bag.

"I see you're still as gallant as ever." She picked up her case. "What's the matter? This too heavy for you?"

"Hey, you set yourself up as Superwoman

— go ahead." He gestured toward her small bag.

"Someday," she heard Ginger say to Ben, "they're both going to wake up and see what this is all about. Thank goodness *we're* through with that nonsense."

The sun was just going down when the car entered the main thoroughfare from the inn. The early dusky light cast shadows on the trees lining the road so that every once in a while as the car twisted and turned in its passage back to the city they went through an eerie patch of paved surface that seemed bordered by ice-clad trees standing sentinel alongside the still, snow-covered highways.

Everyone was silent, and it gave Sheilah a chance to think. Now that everything was out in the open between Simon and her, what would they do? They'd already been through so much, and she didn't know if she wanted to go through it again. She shifted her position so that if she fell asleep, she wouldn't lean against him. But knowing how they felt about each other, how would they avoid each other while working side by side?

Now, that's a problem, she warned herself silently. *That's certainly going to be a problem!*

CHAPTER TEN

Simon pointed to the tape in the editing machine. "Look at this shot, Sheilah — there I am doing my famous ski-slope routine."

"And you said you were an expert skier!" She watched as Simon rolled down a slope.

"Just keep on looking," he said as another scene appeared showing him expertly nego-tiating a long ski run. He grinned. "We faked that last shot just for you. Told you I almost won the big gold. You missed your big chance to learn from an expert."

"Thanks, but no thanks. I don't go in for postgrad courses. I've got my bachelor's in you, remember?"

"But you flunked the course." He left the room.

"We both did," she said quietly and con-tinued to edit the tape, marking with grease pen the scenes she wanted to use. When the footage went black, she carefully rewound it and fast-forwarded it to the shots of Simon and her in the snow; then she flipped the switch to slow motion so that every gesture they made was slowed and exaggerated on the tape — the two of them laughing, throwing snowballs, and casually strolling through the gardens — until finally the last frame focused on the two of them walking at night while the snow swirled around them.

She stopped the tape, freeze-framing the scene. *Simon,* she thought, *you can still charm me. One weekend, and I start having thoughts about you — about us.* She sighed, and touched the lens of the machine as though caressing the picture, leaving smudge marks on the glass.

She turned as Mark entered the room. "I've penciled in the scenes I want," she said. "But I've been careless and dirtied the lens. Sorry."

"No serious damage."

Maybe not to the projector, she thought, *but I wouldn't bet on me.*

She was still thinking about the weekend when Ben joined her in the coffee shop later that morning.

"Last week's figures look good," he said as he sat down. "We're making a dent in the morning ratings thanks to 'Simon Says,' but we still have problems with the six P.M. news. We're third in that time slot."

"I saw that my eleven o'clock is tied for first!"

"Yeah, MacDonald was pleased about that. Says you're doing a great job. Said to tell you."

"Thanks."

"There's Simon and Gretel," Ben said. Sheilah looked behind her just as two elderly women approached Simon. One woman put her hand on his arm, and he bent toward her, smiling, and shook hands with her.

"Look at them," she said. "Women flock to him like metal to a magnet."

"Does it bother you?"

"Me? No! I've already had one go-round with him, remember?"

"So why don't you stop staring at them if it doesn't bother you?" Ben put some change down on the table. "You know, Sheilah, I'm beginning to think Ginger was right about you two — you both overreact when you see each other."

"Just call it a healthy respect for each other, Ben." She rattled a spoon. "Tell me about Ginger. What kind of reviews did she get in Philadelphia?"

"Great ones — what else?" He looked at his watch. "Gotta go."

She gulped the last of her coffee and passed Simon and Gretel on her way out.

"Sheilah." Gretel stopped her. "Your ski-lodge show was really good. Lots of positive viewer reaction. Those shots were fantastic."

"Thank Simon for some of them. He was responsible for directing a couple of scenes."

"I know."

"Did he tell you?"

"Oh, no," Gretel said, shaking her head. "Simon's much too modest to tell me when he's done something good."

"Simon, modest? What an extraordinary verb to use about him!"

"I may even go to the inn — it looked so inviting."

Sheilah looked at her. "Hunting season's over for this year, Gretel." She nodded to both of them. "See you later."

She ran into a last-minute problem with a guest and had to rearrange the schedules to accommodate the change. She was hurrying to tell Mark when Simon stopped her in the hall.

"Why are you so hard on Gretel?" he asked, blocking her way.

"She makes it easy for me. Why are you championing her?"

"Because she's been nice to me."

"I'll bet!"

"Come on, Sheilah." Simon's voice was patient. "I meant it — she's been nice to me. She's been showing me all the high —"

"And low?"

"— spots in town," he continued. "And I heard that remark. Maybe if *you'd* volunteer to guide me around the city. . . ."

"Tours leave every fifteen minutes at the Port Authority. They do a good job too — show you the Empire State Building, Rockefeller Center, and the Statue of Liberty."

"I've already seen them."

"Fifth Avenue?"

"Been there."

"Then I guess you've been just about everywhere."

"That's it? That's the city?"

"Oh, there's lots more — places off the beaten path — streets that only we *cognoscenti* know."

"Show me," he challenged.

She tilted her head and narrowed her eyes. "Okay. Meet me early for breakfast and I'll take you on a tour."

"You've got yourself a date."

"I'm so lucky! But I mean it — *early.*"

He took her at her word and was already waiting at the deli Saturday morning when she got there.

"I really didn't think you'd make it this morning," she apologized, guiding him to a table. "It's such a gloomy day."

Simon looked around the crowded room. "And it's so loud in here."

"You still are a grouch in the morning, aren't you?"

"Me? *Me?*" he asked, his voice in a loud whisper. "You were the one who hated talking before you had your first container of coffee. You were the one who got upset if the paper wasn't at your desk first thing. Remember, love, *you* were the one who was elected office sourpuss of the morning shift. Unanimously, I might add."

"Yes, but, dear heart, you were the one who wound down at three in the afternoon unless you got your afternoon refreshment. All those orange-juice breaks! When I think of how many poor little assistant producers were afraid of you when you pulled your fake hypoglycemic fits!" She took a bite of her bagel. "Let's change the subject. Tell me how the show's going. You know you're the hottest thing in the city these days. I hear women are standing in line for you."

"For my show, you mean."

"That's what they say, but I can tell they'd love to —"

"Why is it," he interrupted, "that when I'm with you, I feel like I'm a bouncing ball?"

"Okay, today'll be my 'be nice to Simon' day. I owe you for the shots you directed, so eat up. It's my treat. We've got a long day ahead." She took another bite of her bagel and motioned to him. "Come on, we've got lots of things to do."

"Okay," she said an hour later as they stood on the corner of Sixth Avenue, "do you want the standard tour guide's spiel or —"

"Why don't you just show me what interests Sheilah Godfrey so much that she thinks this large mass of concrete in any way, shape, or form rivals palm trees and orange groves." His eyes swept the street filled with Saturday-morning shoppers.

"For one thing, it's all real!"

"So's California."

"Sometimes."

"*You* liked it."

"For a while."

"You should have stuck around — it got better."

"For you — not me." She crossed the street with the green light. "Come on, do you want to get run over?" she asked as a taxi turned onto the street.

"Where are we going?"

"Nowhere. We're just walking," she said as Simon's shoulder collided with another man's arm.

"There are too many people."

"Simon, this is your audience." She waved her hand airily. "These people love you."

He squinted his eyes. "Yeah, sure, they

really love me," he said, brushing his coat sleeve. "They really, really love me, just like you do."

"You wanted to see my world? This is it. Anytime you want to call off the tour, say so." She walked ahead of him.

"No way. You can't get rid of me that easily."

They walked a few more blocks, caught up in the crowds of shoppers and browsers. At one street corner a particularly fierce wind whipped around them, and Sheilah shivered and wiped at her nose several times with her handkerchief.

"Cold?" He stamped his feet as they waited for the green light.

"No, you get used to it. It's not always warm sunshine." She dabbed at her nose again and pulled her scarf tighter around her neck.

"You're telling me."

"This is really what I like to do, Simon. I love walking in the crowds — with the crowds."

"You're mad!"

"Oh, I know that people are supposed to hate being crushed and all that, but every time I walk here I keep reminding myself that these are the people I'm putting on the news show for — these are the people who listen and watch. And then I try to get a feel for what interests them. Take that person, for instance." She pointed to a man in a boutique window. "Look at the way everyone's watching him work."

She positioned herself in front of the store window, watching as the man changed the costume on a mannequin. The window dresser, oblivious to the crowd, slipped an antique gray-and-black, heavily beaded dress onto the plastic dummy, adjusted a black jeweled plume in its wig, and faced it out to the people watching. A woman in the audience applauded, and several other watchers took up the rhythm before they began to disperse.

"By this time next week there will be women all over the city looking for copies of that dress," Sheilah said. "I'm interested in who the man is — after all, he's starting a trend — who the people are . . . who will buy the dress . . . and who will be copying the style. See?"

"What I see," he said, gently brushing at the top of her hair, "is a person who's very good at her job."

She touched his hand briefly. "Thanks. Coming from you it's a compliment."

He pulled the collar of his jacket up and around his neck. "Okay, what's next on the agenda?"

"You're sure you want to continue this? It's getting pretty cold." She blew her nose.

"Cold? No, not at all. It's like a summer day," he mocked her, hooking his arm under hers and pulling her along. "I said I was game for this, and I am. Where to, sweetheart? The subway — the bus stop — cab? You name it."

"More walking."

"How far?"

"Not too far. Across the street — Central Park."

"I've seen it."

"At night, maybe, riding in a hansom cab — Gretel's idea, no doubt — but I'll bet you haven't seen it by day." She brushed her cheeks. "Look at it, Simon. Breathe deeply — it's good for you. Fresh air!"

"Exhaust fumes." He looked up at a few scattered snowflakes that had begun falling from the skies. "And snow. They said it would clear up."

She shrugged. "So they goofed. Didn't you ever make a mistake in your life?"

He stopped walking. "Just once."

"Only once? I've made dozens of them."

"Only once when it really mattered." He said it quietly, looking at her, and she frowned.

"Oh, no, Simon Kent. You're not going

serious on me." She sneezed.

"You're catching a cold."

"Not me. I'm indestructible."

"No one's indestructible. Not even you." She sneezed again.

"Lady, I'm not going to be responsible for your catching something. You'd blame me. So let's just call it a day."

"Actually, Simon," she said, wiping her nose again, "I think I will. I'm getting colder by the minute, and I'm not really feeling too well. It began yesterday. I think I may have the flu."

"Then why didn't you say so? Honestly, Sheilah! Why do you persist in keeping up this Superwoman act? I'm taking you home." He put his arm around her. "So much for sight-seeing."

Her apartment was warm, and she leaned back against the cushions of the couch, holding a mug of hot tea, inhaling the steaming aroma while Simon sat across from her, watching her.

"Sorry I don't have any little cakes or stuff to munch on," she said, gesturing toward the kitchen. "I'm always on a semi-diet. Although I do have some crackers and cheese. I'll get them."

"Sit," Simon commanded. "You've been popping up and down since we got here.

You're supposed to rest. And you know I don't like crackers and cheese. Next you'll be offering me those little thin carrot and celery sticks." She winced. "Do you still keep those things in your refrigerator?"

She nodded, then sneezed again.

"I knew it. And I also know you're coming down with something. You still don't know the first thing about taking care of yourself."

"Since when do you know so much about me, and since when have you started caring?" She grimaced, crinkling her face. "Sorry, there I go again."

"You have, without a doubt," he said, handing her a box of tissues, "one of the most tenacious minds and biggest mouths I have ever seen. I told you I've changed. I'm now what people call 'caring.'" He laughed when he saw her shake her head. "Don't you believe me?"

"Does a tiger change its spots?"

"You don't even get your animals right — that's a leopard. Tigers have stripes."

"Like skunks!" She sneezed again and reached for another tissue. "Simon, go home before you catch whatever I have. I'm behind the camera, but you're in front of it."

"Are you going to be okay?"

"Uh-huh. I'm going to go to sleep and see if I can get rid of this cold. When I'm sick, I like to hibernate."

"I remember."

She put out her hand and touched his arm, and he pulled her close to him and held her.

"You take care of yourself," he said quietly.

"I will."

He kissed her forehead. "It's warm."

"I'll be okay."

"I'll call you."

"You don't have to — I'll be all right."

"Hey, this is Simon, remember? This time I promise I'll call — I know the number." He kissed the top of her head. "Go to sleep." He closed the door.

She lay down on her bed, holding her hand on her warm face. *Simon — ah, Simon,* she thought. *If only you were like this five years ago.* She puffed up the pillows on the bed. *I would have stayed with you forever if you'd only cared.*

Gatsby jumped onto the bed and rested his head against her leg. "And I," she said, raising her head to talk to her pet, "would have had someone far different looking than you here beside me." She pulled the blanket around her neck and felt her chilled body begin to relax. She closed her eyes, hoping to rest for a little while, thinking, as she fell asleep, of Simon's gentleness.

She heard the ringing telephone from somewhere within a deep sleep.

"Hello." Her voice was raspy.

"You sound terrible."

"I feel terrible. I'm sleeping."

"Still?"

"What time is it?"

"It's the next day." Simon's voice was gentle.

"Is it really?" She coughed. "I remember getting up and feeding Gatsby and taking him out briefly and then getting back into bed."

"Where you shall remain for the rest of the day."

"How I wish. But I've got to walk Gatsby." She coughed again.

"You can't go out. It's sleeting. And you're sick. Stay right where you are. I'm coming over."

"No, no. I'll be all right."

"Stay there!" he shouted. "I'll be right there."

He brought her the Sunday papers when he arrived a few minutes later, but she shook her head and he put them on the floor next to the bed.

"You look terrible — beautiful, but terrible," he said, touching her forehead. "You're burning up. Get back into bed."

He fastened the leash onto Gatsby's collar. "Come on, pal, you and I are going walking." He looked at her. "And, you, lady, are going back to sleep," he said as she closed her eyes and sank back into the warm bed.

It was already evening when she awoke and heard his voice in the living room. "So what do you think, pal, do we watch the football game or the movie?" Gatsby barked, and as Sheilah smiled she began coughing. The door to the bedroom opened immediately.

"Are you all right?" Simon came into the room.

"Yes. What are you doing here?" Her throat was raw, as though it had been scraped, and she could speak only in a whisper.

"What does it look like? I'm auditioning for the role of a doctor."

"You're crazy," she said in a ragged voice.

"Me? You were the one who played Superwoman. You didn't even have the good sense to come in out of the cold." He felt her cheek. "You're getting cooler. You had the flu."

"And you're going to catch it."

"I never catch anything."

"You're right. You never do. Not even hints."

He shook his head. "Here you are, sick

as a dog — pardon me, Gatsby — and you're still making jokes. Don't you ever give up?" He left the room. "Here," he said reappearing with a tray. "Hungry?"

"What is it?"

"Soup. I made it myself."

"Really?"

"Sure, opened up the can and added water. Eat it. My mother used to say soup was good for you."

"You had a mother? I thought you were spawned." She stirred the soup. "I shouldn't be making fun of you. You saved my life."

"I owed you." The words were soft.

"What for?"

"The tour!" His voice was impatient. "You know perfectly well what for." He rubbed her hand.

"You've wasted your whole weekend on me."

"I had nothing better to do. Besides, I had to think about something, and one place is as good as another."

"Problems?"

"Just something to do with the show. I'll work it out."

"Tell me." She sniffed. "It'll give me a chance just to sit and listen and see how your brain works."

"Another crack?"

"You're getting paranoid about it." She dabbed at her nose. "When I make a crack about your brains, you'll know it. Besides, I never was really impressed with your mind. I can't remember one particularly cogent thing you ever said to me." She pulled the blankets around her, and he got up to adjust them at the foot of the bed.

"No? Your brain wasn't exactly perking along, either, as I recall. What did you ever say to impress me?" He bent his head, fixing the afghan.

"I said good-bye." She said the words softly.

He paused and then slowly nodded his head.

"Yep, you sure did." He gave the blanket an extra tug. "And see what it's gotten you — a hospital orderly."

"Simon," she said, relieved that the moment of intimacy had passed, "come sit down and talk to me. What's the problem?"

"No problem. Just a personnel change. My producer's going back to the Coast — he's been offered a sitcom."

"Nice. And — ?"

"Well, Diana, a friend of mine, heard about it, and she called me a couple of days ago and asked to be considered for the job."

"Diana? As in the woman you knew

way back when?"

"Yes."

She coughed. "Then it's a personal problem. I can't help you."

"It isn't a personal problem — it's a professional one."

"Not the way I hear it. Isn't she the one you were chasing madly around the entire state of California when I left?"

"Not the entire state. And at least she was there. You weren't, remember? You were on another coast. Something, it seems, got in the way of our relationship."

"That something, as you put it so casually, Simon, is precisely why you and I could never get together for any long-term commitment. That something was a job offer here at the station. It was my career that was on the line, in case you hadn't noticed."

"I thought you were doing well out there — you were being groomed for a producer's job."

"Which was offered to me here. Or didn't you think I should take this job?"

"That wasn't it."

"All right then, what was it?"

"You really want to know?" He rocked back and forth on the edge of the bed. "I didn't think you were ready for it."

She blinked. "What? I'm a good producer."

"You grew into it."

"I sure did. But that's not the issue." She strained her voice, and it got raspier.

"Here," he said handing her a glass of water.

She sipped it slowly. "Thanks. So you didn't think I deserved the job, huh? How's that for faith?"

"It was more than that, and you know it."

"Ah, now comes the moment of truth. You were jealous?"

"Aw, come on, Sheilah, that's crazy!"

"Is that why you didn't want me to take a producing job out there? You couldn't take it if I succeeded? You needed me around full-time to massage your ego?"

"What I couldn't take, Sheilah, if you really want to know, was the fact that I thought you were being pushed too soon. I didn't want to see you fail. It would have devastated you."

"Have I ever failed?" She shredded a tissue.

"No."

"Then why'd you think that? Why should that have worried you?"

"Because despite our differences, and despite our running around and away from each other and avoiding anything that reeked of permanence and all that stuff . . . I did have an inkling that I was falling in love with you, and I didn't want you hurt."

"You never told me that."

"No commitments, remember?"

"But you could have said something."

"No, I couldn't. We both had to get on with our careers first. Then, if something happened and we stayed together, there would have been time."

She wiped at her watery eyes so that red circles rimmed them. "Well, we didn't stay together, did we?"

"No . . . no, we didn't." He got up from the bed. "Want something else to drink?"

"Please."

He handed her a glass of juice.

"No comments," he said as she started to smile when she saw the orange liquid.

"None whatsoever." She drank it and handed the glass back to him. "Okay, now back to your problem."

He sat down again.

"Mind if I ask you a personal question?" She cleared her throat.

He smiled. "I'm an adult — ask me anything."

"All right. What makes it a problem? Is it Diana? Is it your entanglement with her? Or what?"

"Diana and I are through — we have been

for years. Whatever was between us then is long over. She's got someone else in her life now. That's the reason she wants to come East — her friend's being transferred here."

"Well, is it that you have some feelings for her that makes it a problem for you?"

"Good heavens, no!" He looked at her with narrowed eyes. "How can you even ask that?"

I had to, Simon, she thought, crumpling the blanket in her hands. *I wanted to know.* . . . "Then," she said aloud, "why don't you want to hire her — give her a chance?"

"Because she's not right for the show. She's great on hard-core news, but she's wrong for 'Simon Says.' "

"Couldn't she learn?"

"No, it wouldn't work. She's as stubborn as you, and she has very definite ideas about what works — and I admit they work well in news programming. But she doesn't have" — he paused, drumming his fingers on the blanket — "the best word I can think of is 'heart.' If we run an issue-oriented program she's fine, but when the issue becomes people and what happens to them, she loses it."

"You're being harsh. Maybe she's changed."

He continued to drum on the bed. "I was out there until a few weeks ago, and I didn't

145

see any change. And, frankly, suppose she does come out here on my say-so and she doesn't work out? Then what?"

"She gets another job. Or you help her, or —"

"Or I live with my mistakes," he finished the sentence. He shook his head quickly. "I've learned to live with a lot of my mistakes but . . . no, she wouldn't work out."

She leaned back and closed her eyes.

"You're tired," he said. "Go back to sleep. I'll stay for a couple of hours in case you need me."

"One, I won't need you — and, two, I'm thinking."

Simon pressed his lips together and wrinkled his brow. "While you're thinking, think about this: How'd you like to produce 'Simon Says'?"

"What?" She opened her eyes.

"You heard me. How would you like to produce my show?"

"You're kidding!"

He shook his head slowly.

"You're not kidding?" She tugged at the covers, and it was her turn to shake her head. "Thanks, but no thanks. I wouldn't even consider it. It's not my kind of job — and besides, it would never work."

"Why not?"

"Well, for starters, I'm a news hound — you know that. I've been in news and news features for a long while, and I really love it." She blew her nose again. "Two, I enjoy my job. I've got a great crew . . . we all get along . . . we all have the same ideas about news features. And, three, quite frankly, I'm top dog in my spot. True, it may be a little spot — certainly nothing compared to your show — but I'm happy with it for now."

She leaned her head to one side. "You're a different animal, Simon. You're doing global stuff — talking to people from all over the world. I'm not into that right now. I'm still trying to figure out what the little person, that person in the middle of the street outside my window, thinks. Your show is different."

"Producing's producing."

"Really? And all interviewers are the same?" She arched an eyebrow.

"Okay, I get it. That was a stupid thing to say. Of course it isn't. But how can you refuse my offer? I think this would be the perfect job for you — a great break."

"A break?" The word made her pause, and it seemed as though she was reminding herself of other days.

"Sure. You've got to move up sometime."

"I'm doing rather nicely by myself, thank you."

147

"But this would be a major boost for you."

She shook her head slowly.

"You don't think so?"

"No, that's not what I'm thinking," she said quietly. "I'm thinking, if you must know, that you're doing it again! You're pressuring me . . . making decisions for me . . . pushing me to do what you want me to do." She peered at him.

"Uh-uh. I'm just telling you that you'll get exposure — *national* exposure — if you take over the show."

"If I take over Simon Kent's show."

"Yeah, sure it's my show — but you'd be the producer."

"Simon, love, read my lips since you can't hear my voice. I really thank you, but I don't think I want the job. I like what I'm doing. I've got all sorts of ideas for my show."

"Use them on mine."

"They're not your type."

"Then think of some ideas for me." He picked up her hand and squeezed it, and she saw the excitement shining in his eyes. "Come on, Sheilah, think about it."

"But I really don't want it." She slumped against the pillows. "All right, I'll think about it. We'll talk about it some other time."

"Next week," he pressed.

"Okay."

"I'm serious. I'll talk to Mac about it — smooth the way. After all," he said, smiling, "you told me I was the hottest thing around."

"Your humility, Simon, is overwhelming. Let me sleep on it for a couple of days. Right now I'm a bit foggy." She closed her eyes again.

"Go back to sleep. I'll stick around for a while, feed Gatsby, take him for a walk, and then go home. Don't worry about the door, I'll lock it. And if you need me, just call. This time I'll come." He ruffled her hair. "Good grief! You still look terrible."

CHAPTER ELEVEN

Ben came into her office the next morning while she was trying to put together the week's programming.

"Heard you've been sick."

"Who told you?" Sheilah wiped at her still red nose.

"Simon."

"Did he tell you he performed yeoman duty this weekend? Saved my life." She blue-penciled a paragraph.

"Well, I've got some news for you that should make you feel better." Ben twirled his seat from side to side.

"Make my day." She put down the pencil.

"Mac wants to talk to you when you have a chance."

"About what?" she sneezed and reached for a tissue.

"Producing 'Simon Says.' "

She narrowed her eyes. "Simon's spoken to him already?"

"Yeah. It's a terrific job."

"I know, but I wanted more time to think about it."

"What's to think about? It's a great break for you."

She felt a pain begin in the back of her head, and she twisted her neck in an effort to relieve the tension.

Ben noticed the movement. "You want it, don't you?"

"I don't know. I told Simon I needed more time — that I had some reservations about it. I know it's —" She pressed her hands into the base of her skull, massaging it.

"Well, I wouldn't think about it too long, Sheilah. Look at it this way — it's a plum assignment. Do you know how many people would give their eyeteeth to get this job? We'd have lines into the street if they knew the job was open. This is the big one, Sheilah — a gigantic boost up the ladder."

She licked her dry lips. "Those words sound vaguely familiar. Like Simon said them. . . ."

"Well," Ben muttered, looking away, "maybe he did say something like that. But it's true. And you deserve the chance."

"He's convinced you, hasn't he?" The isolated pain gave way to a full-blown headache.

"He's trying to help you. Why are you hesitating?"

"Oh . . ." she said, taking a bottle of

151

aspirin from her desk drawer, "it's probably nothing. Just me being extra cautious. What kind of concessions can I get?"

"Like what?" He doodled on a notepad.

"I'd like to take Beth with me. And Mark. And I'd like to make some arrangements for my crew and some other things — like money . . . responsibilities. . . ." She put the tablet in her mouth and washed it down with cold coffee.

Ben watched her and made a face when she swallowed. "Why don't you talk to Mac first, and then we can work out all those details."

"What you're saying, Ben, is that you and Mac and Simon," she said, stumbling on the last name, "have already discussed a lot of these so-called details and that I'm not to worry about anything." The pain shifted and centered above her eyes.

"Something like that." He ripped the notepaper. "I'd get on it as soon as possible, Sheilah."

The conversation with Mac had been fairly brief, and now, sitting in her own office, she had time to think about the offer. She swung her chair around toward the window, looking down and watching the people walking in the street.

You know it really is a break for you, she told herself. *It's what you want — recognition. It's what careers are all about in this business.* She tapped the chair arms. "But is it?" she said aloud. "What about my plans for my own show someday? Using my own ideas?" She rubbed at her temples — at the dull pain that continued to ache despite two aspirins. She knew they were excuses. What was the real problem? Why all the doubts? *Why do I have the feeling that I'm being pushed into something I don't think I want — that Simon is running interference for me again?* she asked herself. She swung her chair around and remembered the conversation she had had with Mac.

"We think this is the perfect move for you, Sheilah," he had said. "You've got good ideas — you know Simon and his ways — and producing his show would give you national exposure and experience. I don't mind telling you that when Simon suggested you, I may have had some doubts — I like the local work you're doing on the eleven-o'clock news. And I wasn't sure whether you'd want the job — I know you like news. But then, you're ambitious. And when Simon assured me he had spoken to you about it — Well, that was it. He's a good man, Sheilah — has a lot of talent. And when he told me that you'd be just great in this job, I didn't have a minute's hesitation after that — he hasn't built his reputation on failures. Look at his ratings!"

Sheilah drew imaginary circles on her desk blotter.

Why hadn't she just told him she was happy with the news? Why hadn't she just said, "I know, Mac, and thank you for your faith in me, but I really want to stay where I am for now — I'm comfortable with it and I have all sorts of ideas to improve it."

"Why didn't I just say no?" she asked aloud.

"Say no?" Ben asked as he came through the door. "You didn't turn it down, did you?"

"No."

"Good. With all the heavy hitters — Mac, Simon — going to bat for you? Hey, it's more power and more money for you. And don't forget the prestige of working on the show — you're bound to get more attention on 'Simon Says.' Let's face it, news shows are on every local station, and unless you're doing a fantastic job, no one really notices the credits too much."

"That's not true, Ben," she protested. "I've gotten some nice notes from network people."

"All enclosing their cards, telling you to

get in touch with them in a year or so, but never a firm 'come see me' request. Right?" He played with a rubber band on her desk.

"Right."

"That's the way this business is. Oh, sure, one of them might remember you when you call in a couple of years looking for an upward spot on the networks, but usually those cards are sent to anyone and everyone who looks like a potential winner. And that's the key word: potential. They're always on the lookout for the next national news broadcaster or the next sports personality. It's the nature of this business."

"You're right. What can I say?"

"Say you're happy about the job. You are, aren't you?" The rubber band snapped and stung his finger. "Is something bothering you about all this?"

"You're pretty sharp, Ben. But it's probably me being extra-crazy from the flu."

"It's a great move for you. Working with Simon is going to be great for your career. You won't regret it."

Okay, Sheilah, old girl, she thought after Ben left, *you know what the problem is — it's Simon. He's taking over your personal and professional life again. It's five years ago all over. . . .*

She looked out the window once more.

Okay, so it was Simon. But this time she'd be on her guard. And, she admitted, it really was a good job.

Simon was genuinely happy about her decision.

"Sit here," he said, pointing to a chair, "and let me tell you why I need you — why I want you on board." He stood in front of her. "What I want to do is more pertinent issues. They could be global and international stuff — but I want them on issues dealing with life as it is here and now."

He put his hands together. "Like you, I want to get into people's minds and find out what they're worrying about. Oh, sure, I can pick any topic out of the air — the budget, politics — and it will make sense to some people and certainly everyone will have an opinion on it. But there are times when I'm sitting on stage or walking around the studio asking questions and I sense that the audience is just asking or answering questions out of habit." His eyes narrowed as he squinted. Sheilah remembered the gesture from the past.

"You're not saying they're not interested?" She looked at him with disbelief.

"No, they're interested, but it just doesn't

pertain to them. It's not their problem. The big things — war, disease, peace — people feel strongly about them, one way or another, but —"

"But sometimes the person in the audience is more concerned about how he's going to pay this month's rent or if his kid is getting into drugs or trouble and how he can prevent it."

"Exactly."

"That drug program you did in California —"

"Someone on the staff had a friend who was worried about his son."

"That's what I did on the news show. I let the viewers know we were concerned about everyday problems — *their* problems. The big ones they can't do much about except protest, but the little ones — the everyday problems — those they may be able to change."

"You've got it." He sat down beside her.

"So what would my job be — besides the general producing of the show?"

"Come up with that kind of ideas! I'll help, but I need another idea person on the show. That's why I wasn't keen on Diana taking the job — she's great at production, but ideas about the person in the street aren't her forté."

"And they are mine."

"You practically told me that last weekend." He looked at her and smiled. "You sure were exciting last weekend."

"Even with my cold? Tell me how much freedom I'll have to make the choices."

"Pretty much, although I want input on them."

"Do I have to clear them with anyone?"

"Only me." He pushed at his shirtsleeves.

She touched her lips with her thumb. "Suppose we don't agree?"

"We can work it out."

"You're sure?"

"Yeah." He got up and walked around her again. "Then that's it. We're both comfortable with this? We can work together? It's going to be like old times again for us, I know it. Just like old times."

"Yes," she agreed, trying hard to ignore the feathery ticklings of uncertainty she felt at her temples. "Yes," she repeated, "just like old times."

CHAPTER TWELVE

Simon had his feet propped up on the desk in front of him, his body relaxed in a back-tilted upholstered desk chair and his head resting on his arms on the headpiece.

"So that's what a successful TV host does in the morning."

"No way, Sheilah. This is the first chance I've had to relax. Look at all this." He pointed to a large pile of papers on his desk. "I have to go through this by tonight. Every one of these people wants to be on the show, and I've got to decide which public-relations offices have done the best job for their clients and have interested me enough to want to see more." He riffled through some of the top papers.

"Try doing the news show someday and having to work on deadline. What are these?" She picked up the top sheet of the pile.

"A bio on someone — oh, yeah, America's latest teen idol." He mimicked a rock guitarist. "They all sound alike."

"And you're beginning to sound your age. Just because all these young things were born after you and are making a mint, you shouldn't criticize. You're just getting old, dear one."

"Not too old to appreciate a good-looking woman when I see one." He playfully lunged at her as she sidestepped out of his reach.

"Simon, really! Act your age."

"I'm trying to."

"You know that attempt you just made doesn't even merit a sexual harassment charge." She made a clicking sound. "Poor Simon. One of the worst things to witness is the deterioration of a legend."

"Deterioration, my foot! Honey, what I've deteriorated, no other man even has. Anyway, what do you want?"

"A list of all the people who are scheduled for the show in the next month, so I won't duplicate when I begin scheduling."

"I'll get it to you. How's it going?"

"Okay, so far. I'm enjoying it. I like meeting the guests."

He eyed the stack of press releases. "For the first fifty, you will." He swung his feet off the desk and reached for his jacket. "I'll see you downstairs."

She met him later at the back of the set. It was ten minutes to airtime. She pointed to the audience.

"I'm amazed at how calm you are."

"I've done this for three years now." He

tugged at his shirtsleeves.

"But still — a different audience every day . . . a different guest and a different topic."

"After a while, you get the hang of it. And besides, if everyone does his job right, the guests are primed, they're interesting, and the audience goes with it. Watch," he said to her. "You'll see what I mean. Forget my pessimism this morning, I was just over-tired and overworked. This is really fun."

He straightened his tie, grinned at her, and went into the studio. "Hello, how are you today?" she heard him ask as she ducked into the video booth where Mark was di-recting the cameras.

"We've got a few more minutes," Mark said as she sat at the terminals watching through the monitors as Simon interacted with the audience.

"How many of you ever heard about nou-velle cuisine?" he asked. "Come on, raise your hands," he coaxed, and the audience started to laugh. "I know you've heard of it, and if you haven't, you should. It's good for your health." He stopped in front of a thin woman. "Tell me," he said, leaning toward her with the microphone, "do you eat nouvelle cuisine?" The woman laughed shyly, and the audience responded with more giggles as Simon walked back on the stage.

"He makes it seem so easy," Mark said, signaling another camera angle. "He's a master at this, Sheilah. Look at the way he and the audience work together. Not just verbally, but the body language too. That's communication!"

"Uh-huh." She glanced at the clock. "Two minutes to go."

"Well," Simon said, walking toward a man standing at the corner of the stage, "this gentleman just wrote a book about nouvelle cuisine, and he tells us that if we all eat it and if we follow some of his rules, we're all going to get thin." He shook the man's hand. "And if anyone can help me control my weight," he said, mocking his own trim figure, "then I'm going to listen." He sat down in a chair opposite his guest and then looked up at the booth and winked at Sheilah.

"Five . . . four . . . three . . . two . . . one. . . . It's party time," Mark said calmly, and she watched as the red lights of the cameras blinked and he began giving orders to the camera people.

The show went smoothly and quickly, and Sheilah was surprised when she heard Mark's "That's a wrap," ending the program.

"He's pure gold for the station," Mark said. "Solid fourteen carat. A pro all the way. We're going to like it here, Sheilah — it's a chance of a lifetime to work with him." Mark opened the door for her. "He's a great talent."

She knew that the nominations for the local TV awards had been announced that afternoon. When she arrived back at her office, there was a huge bouquet of bronze and gold chrysanthemums on her desk.

"For you," Beth said. "There's a card attached."

Sheilah opened the small white envelope.

Congratulations! she read. *But then I always thought you were a winner. Simon.*

She read the card a second time as the phone rang.

"Well, you really did it, didn't you?" His voice was deep, sincere.

"It's only a nomination, Simon, but thanks for the flowers. They're my favorites."

"I know. I remembered."

She traced the edge of a fluffy petal with her finger. *Sometimes,* she thought, *you make me remember too much.* "Thanks," she said aloud.

"For sending the flowers — or for remembering?"

"For both," she said softly.

Simon seemed particularly playful with his

audience the next day. He told them funny jokes, recited anecdotes about his childhood, and remembered his early days in broadcasting. The men and women in the studio responded with laughter and applause.

"You can feel the electricity in there," Mark said, adjusting a monitor. "They're primed."

"Uh-huh. Three minutes," Sheilah said into her mike, and Simon nodded. He was already seated on the stage with his guest when suddenly he snapped his fingers and spoke to the studio audience.

"Friends," he said, "I want to introduce you to a new member of our show — Sheilah Godfrey." He pointed to her in the control booth, and she nodded to the audience. "Sheilah's the new producer of 'Simon Says,' so if you have any complaints, call her. If you just want to compliment us, then, naturally, call me."

"Simon dear," Sheilah said, speaking softly into the mike connected to his ear wire, "if you ever do that again, I'll blow your ratings way up with my comments."

He began to laugh and pointed to his earpiece. "Sheilah's yelling at me for embarrassing her," he told the audience just as Mark signaled "on the air." Simon went smoothly into the introduction of his guest.

164

"You know, looking at him and listening to him, you would think he agrees with that woman, wouldn't you?" Mark was adjusting the monitoring screen. "Actually, he's miles away from her in thoughts and ideals, but he never lets on. He doesn't even bait her. Merely lets her talk and then lets the audience make up their own minds. And they sure do. You never know what their reaction is until you hear the questions. And it's amazing, but he doesn't manipulate them. That's what makes him such a good host, Sheilah — he really respects the audience. He's got feelings — sensitivity — whatever. He's got it."

Mark bent down to the screen, not seeing her skeptical face. "He can make anyone look good. But you already knew that, didn't you? You worked with him before in California."

CHAPTER THIRTEEN

Sheilah pushed open the door to Simon's office. "Are we really going to have that gossip columnist on the show?"

"Yeah. Watch the ratings soar. People love celebrity rumors."

"Speaking of rumors, I haven't seen Gretel lately. Have you?"

He closed one eye. "Getting personal?"

"Of course not. What you do with your life has nothing to do with me."

"Maybe it should."

"No way, Simon. Those days are gone forever. So where's Gretel?"

"On vacation."

"With whom?"

"How should I know?"

"I heard rumors."

He looked at the picture of the gossip columnist. "You listen to rumors, Sheilah? *You?*"

She slid down in her chair. "I'm only human."

He winked again, and she threw a paper clip at his chest.

"You know," he said, "there are a million

women like Gretel. If you really looked at her, you would see she's lonely."

"That's a ploy — chapter one on how to get a man." She scraped at her nail polish.

"No ploy, Sheilah. She's a nice person — just lonely."

"You fell for it, didn't you?"

"I 'fell for it,' as you so bluntly put it, because I know it's the truth — everyone is lonely at some time in his life." He snapped the clip and looked at her. "What about you?"

"Me? Lonely? Haven't got time for it. Besides, I have Gatsby, and all I have to give him is a bone."

"Instead of — ?"

"My heart." She grinned. "Much easier on me. And he's warm on cold evenings."

"So am I."

"If you say so."

"I can prove it."

She pushed away from the desk. "I didn't come here to discuss your love life."

"It could be yours. . . ." He leered at her.

"Enough!"

"Have it your own way. Did you want something when you came bursting in here?"

"You still want the lady gossip?"

"Like I said, she makes a good guest."

"Okay," she said, irritated at his choice. "It's your show."

Simon put down a pencil. "We all have input."

"But you have the final say."

"Only because I have to do the interviewing and —"

"And the show carries your name."

"And my reputation."

"So, like I said a few minutes ago, it's your show." She looked at her watch. "I've still got a lot of work."

The studio audience was noisy that morning. Most of the people wanted to appear before the camera and called out to Simon when he passed them, hoping to get his attention.

"I have a question, Simon." A woman stood up and tucked her purse on the seat.

"Okay, ask it." Simon put the mike in front of her.

"Camera one on the lady," Mark said.

"Is it a question about relationships for my guest?"

"No," the woman said, shaking her head, "it's about you. Here you are, a good-looking man, fine dresser, talented, and you obviously make a lot of money —"

"Uh-oh," Mark said, "here it comes. I knew there'd be a little old lady with this kind of question. Keep the camera on both of them — I have a feeling, Sheilah, we're going to get a terrific reaction shot of Simon shortly." Sheilah edged her chair closer to the monitor screen. "Watch this. Simon's already sensing the question."

"So what I'm asking is this," the woman continued, "how come someone like you isn't married? How come we never read about you and somebody?" The woman looked around. "There are all sorts of beautiful women here in the audience, and I see lots of lovely women who work on your show. Why don't you ever date any of them?"

"Because I've been waiting for you all my life," Simon answered glibly, taking the microphone away from the woman.

"No, answer it, Simon," the guest relationship-expert said from the stage. "Are you afraid to answer it?"

Simon cleared his throat, obviously uncomfortable. "I'm not afraid to answer it. Uh, let me see," he began. "You want me to be honest, right?"

"Yes," the audience shouted.

"Okay," he said, sitting down on the edge of the stage, facing them. "I've been involved in several relationships that haven't worked out. For one reason or another, they just weren't what I wanted . . . or what I was looking for. I wanted my freedom — I enjoyed it — I liked being able to pick up and go where and when . . . and with whom I wanted to. And — and I know this might sound arrogant or conceited, but . . . as far as giving all that up — Well, I never did meet a woman who seemed worth it to me." He ducked his head as he heard the audience murmur and laugh. "Hey," he said, smiling, "you did ask me to be honest, didn't you?" He looked toward the production booth.

"He wants a commercial right now. Can we go for it?" Mark turned to Sheilah.

"Yes, go to black." Mark signaled to Simon, and she was glad he didn't look at her and see her anger. *Thanks, Simon,* she seethed inwardly. *At least now I know what you always thought.* She watched as he recovered his momentum. Within a few moments he had the audience directing questions to his guest.

The rest of the show ran smoothly, and when Mark called for the final credits, he snapped his fingers.

"This one was a winner, Sheilah. One of the few times I ever saw Simon at a loss for words. The audience loved it. And speaking of the devil — hi, Simon."

She turned and saw him standing at the door, and she arched an eyebrow.

"Hey," he said to her, "about today's show

— uh, I think I owe you an apology."

She shrugged. "You owe a lot of women apologies. Forget it, Simon. Besides, it was interesting to hear about all your other relationships." She pushed back her chair. "How many were there? You made it sound like you held a lottery every so often. Pick four numbers, ladies, and Simon Kent will choose the winner. A thin dime will get you a spin around the block with the man of your dreams."

"That's not what I meant. It just came out wrong." He ran his hand through his hair. "You know there's no telling when you go live what's going to be asked."

"Or what you're going to answer. It's amazing what you can find out on the air. Beats educational TV."

"Cut it out, Sheilah. I thought it was a pretty good show in spite of that question. What did you think?"

She glared at him and walked close to him so that their faces were almost touching. "You want to know what I think?" she asked. "I think you're a real jerk. I think all your ex-girlfriends should form a club. I think we could call ourselves Simple Simon's Sweethearts." She pushed past him. "Excuse me, but next time you don't have to be that honest. Lie a little."

"It was only in fun."

She started to open the door of the control booth but instead turned and faced him again.

"I didn't hear anyone laughing, Simon. So we're all unworthy, are we? Tell me, did it ever occur to you that people might have gotten hurt — that the end of a romance could be painful? No! But all those ladies out there think poor Simon has had a string of bad luck — he's never met someone who measured up. Tune in tomorrow, folks, for the next exciting chapter of Simon Kent's life. Who's your guest tomorrow, Simon? Santa Claus? Maybe you should reveal all about him too!"

"Hey, I'm sorry. It was only a flip remark."

"No, I think for once in your life you told the truth."

He stepped toward her and took her hand gently, holding it for a brief moment.

"I wouldn't hurt you, Sheilah, and I would never, *never* make flip remarks about you. Believe me."

"You just did, Simon. And in front of all your millions of syndicated viewers. Let's just forget it."

For two days they avoided each other, each leaving notes or having their assistants relay messages.

172

Sheilah read the memo Beth handed her. "Simon left it here. Said to give it to you as soon as you got back from lunch."

Sheilah put down the paper. "He wants to make a substitution for this week. Did you tell him he can't do that on such short notice?"

"No, how could I? It's his show."

"Well, he just can't go around making last-minute changes like this. I had everything lined up. He's giving us only two days' notice." She reread the note. "Who is this man, anyhow? I haven't heard of him, have you?" She was already dialing Simon's office.

"Look," she said when he answered, "you just can't go and change guests on me like this. There isn't enough time."

"Sure there is." His voice was lazy. "Besides, he's in the news."

"Who is he?"

"You haven't heard of him? He's new money. He's the guy who's about to make a fortune with a new movie he's producing."

"And for him we're taking off a government official?"

"Reschedule the official. This producer is going to be in town for only a couple of days. I met him at a party. He's interesting, and the movie is supposed to be sensational."

"Sensational or not, we can't reschedule

173

like this." She tried to keep her voice even.

"Sure we can."

"No, we can't."

"Sheilah, just do it, please. For me," he said, and when she didn't answer, he added curtly, "Sheilah, just do it. Make our apologies and offer to get the official a room at a hotel. Emergencies are written into the budget."

"And this is an emergency?"

"That's right!" His voice was terse. She slammed the phone down. "Simon says to do it, Beth, so we do it. It's his show." She felt her throat constrict, and for a few seconds she jabbed hard at the push button numbers of the phone, silently pounding them, releasing her anger. Finally she jammed her entire hand over all the numbers.

"Are you all right?" Beth asked.

"Just very angry, Beth." She reached for her coat. "I've got an appointment," she lied, "and it's going to take all afternoon. If anyone wants me, I'll be in tomorrow."

She walked out into the cold air, taking huge gulps of it into her lungs, breathing deeply in an effort to relax herself. *That's it!* she thought. *I should never have taken this job with him. I didn't want it in the first place. I was happy in news.* She crossed the street to the bus stop, glad of the opportunity to wait in line among strangers. *If I'd only listened to myself, I wouldn't be in this position. I should have just stayed away from him.*

She got off the bus and decided to cut across the park to her apartment. When a gust of cold wind suddenly whirled around her, she wrapped her scarf even tighter around her neck and walked faster through the winding paths until she came to an empty bench. She sat down and ran her finger across the back of the wooden bench and watched as a pigeon flew by. The bird approached a woman who sat nearby methodically flinging popped corn on the browned grass for the birds.

"I do this every day," the woman said, reaching into a plastic shopping bag.

"Don't you ever get tired of it?"

The woman seemed to recoil at the question. "Of feeding the pigeons? No," she answered, revealing a large gap where her front teeth should have been. "Birds are my friends." She extended the grocery bag to her. "Want some?"

"No, thanks."

"I know them all by name." She pointed to a fat gray bird. "That one is the kingpin. He lets everyone know he's boss. Watch him. He struts around, puffing out his chest — just like some people." She threw a few kernels of corn to the bird. "But he's my favorite, and I think he knows it. Know what I mean?"

Sheilah nodded her head. "I'm afraid I do." She started to rise as several more birds began to surround the older woman.

"Come by any day. I'm always here."

Sheilah smiled at the old woman, then started on her way. She hunched her shoulders and lowered her head against a particularly frigid blast of wind as she turned down Seventy-fourth Street.

She should have known it was going to turn out like this, she thought, walking up the steps to her building. She should never have let Simon into her apartment that night, let alone her heart. She stopped on the step, paralyzed by the thought. Her heart? She inserted the key into the outer door. *You knew better,* she scolded herself silently. *Now that's only problem number one. Problem number two is that you're going to have to figure a way to get this job back on track, or else it's going to be like California again. You knew better, Sheilah. You knew better and you blew it.*

She went into her apartment. She should have stayed with the news. Why did she let them talk her into this job? She sat down on the couch, still wrapped in her coat and scarf, and stroked Gatsby. Simon! Why didn't he stay in California? She tickled the dog's ears. "Well, pal," she began and then stopped. "See what he's done to us, Gatsby? I'm already calling you pal, like he does. It seems Simon does get his way — in everything — eventually." She slowly unwound her scarf and let it fall to the floor, all the while shaking her head and thinking about Simon.

CHAPTER FOURTEEN

They met in the elevator coming into work, and aside from the required "Good morning," neither of them spoke again until the elevator stopped at their floor and they got out.

"About yesterday," Simon began as they stepped into the corridor leading to their offices. "I —"

"Forget it, Simon. It was minor," she lied. Why give him the satisfaction of knowing how upset she'd been?

"That suits me." They walked in silence so that the only sound heard in the hall was that of her heels as they clicked on the tiled floor. "Sure you're not angry?" he asked again, rubbing his arms. "It's awfully chilly in here."

"I'm not angry."

"I'm glad to hear that — I can imagine what it's like when you are."

She stopped abruptly, turning to face him. "Look, Simon, I've got a lot of things on my mind. And I've got to soothe a bumped politician, remember?"

He winced. "Okay — so I —" He nodded to a secretary coming out of an office. "Look, let's not talk about that now. It's over and done with. Let's change the subject."

She sniffed. "Whatever you want."

"Are you going to the awards ceremonies?"

"That's a quick change. Of course I'm going to the dinner." She hurried her pace.

"So am I." He tapped a wall with his newspaper.

"You? What for? You weren't involved in locals last year."

"They asked me to be a presenter."

"I should have known. The big hero comes to town!" She waved her handbag. "For what category?"

"Local news."

"That's mine!"

"I know. I was going to surprise you."

"You have."

They turned a corner in the hall. "No, I mean when we got there."

She stopped walking again. "What do you mean, when *we* got there?"

He grinned at her. "That's another thing I forgot to tell you. We're going together."

She leaned against a wall and looked him straight in the eye. "How do you figure that? I don't recall asking you to accompany me."

"You didn't. I volunteered."

"I don't need volunteers, thank you."

"Actually, Mac asked me to go with you."

She narrowed her eyes. "Doesn't he think I can get there by myself?"

"Whew! You are burned about yesterday, aren't you?"

She took a deep breath. "I don't like being ordered to do something."

"Maybe I did come across too strong," he conceded.

"Maybe you did. Anything else?"

"Yeah."

"What?"

"Wear something blue to the ceremonies — I've always liked blue." He winked at her and went into his office and she continued looking at his doorway.

I remember, Simon, she thought, and then sighed. *Didn't I always wear something blue for you?*

They met by accident once more that afternoon as he came out of the studio. She was reading copy, her eyes downcast, when she bumped into him.

"I'm sorry —" she began and then said, "oh, it's you."

He smiled and picked up the papers she had dropped. "We really have to stop meeting like this. People will talk."

"It won't work this time, Simon. Don't try to cajole me."

"Whoa — still burned. Okay, have it your way. Did you get the memo I put on your desk?"

"About what?" She shifted the stack of papers in her hands.

"About close-ups of me. Try not to call for so many of them, will you? I'd rather my guests and the audience get the camera more often."

"Why? The TV audience wants to see you — that's why they tune in." She was impatient to get back to her office.

"But I think they'd like to see the guests' reactions too."

"That's Mark's job — he's the director. He calls the camera angles."

"He told me you've been calling for more shots of me. You're the producer." His voice was clipped, and she felt the cold weight at the back of her neck that she knew signaled the beginning of another headache.

"It's a wonder you remembered. Okay, I'll do what you want. You're the head honcho on the show."

"Come on, Sheilah," he said, looking uneasily about the studio, "give it up. I'm just trying to do what's best for the viewers."

"Or what *you* think is best for them."

"I've been on the show a lot longer than —"

She tilted her head. "Than I have? You're right. Anything else you want?"

"Hey," he suggested, "let's call a truce. This isn't getting either of us anywhere. I'm not questioning your production skills. Heck, I was the one who wanted you — who suggested you to Mac — who asked for you. Remember?"

"I remember that all too well." She shook her head so that the soft bangs fell in front of her eyes. "Am I supposed to be grateful for the rest of my life?"

His eyes glinted. "What's that supposed to mean?"

"You figure it out."

"I don't have to — nor do I want to. Look, all I'm doing is trying to have a professional discussion with you, not create a war. I'm telling you what I think." He lowered his voice as a production assistant passed them.

"It's the way you express your opinion, Simon. It's like you're giving orders. I don't take those whether it's your show or not. Frankly, it comes across too much like everything has to be run past you for your final say. We're professionals too, you know."

"Then, for Pete's sake," he said angrily as he pushed the door to the studio, "why don't you act like one?"

Her anger continued throughout that evening. The next day Sheilah was already in the control booth with her notes when Mark arrived.

"Early, aren't you?" He looked at the clock.

"I wanted to go over some changes with you. Go with more shots of the audience and the guests instead of Simon, will you?"

"Sure." Mark turned a knob, testing the monitoring screen. "Simon already talked to me about it." He flicked another switch. "That guy has a knack of knowing just what's right for his audience. But then," he added, "that's why he's on top."

"I think," she said as she tapped the blue pencil she was holding, "I've heard enough of Simon's ability to gauge an audience." She tightened her fingers around the pencil and pressed it onto the paper, pushing it so hard that it cracked and broke in half. She picked up the two pieces and angrily threw them onto the table.

"I'm sorry, Mark, discount it," she apologized immediately. "I've had some things on my mind." She rubbed at her forehead, trying to erase the band of pain that encircled her head.

"No trouble — no trouble at all, Sheilah. We all have days like that," he said as the camera crew came into the studio and took their places in front of the equipment. "We're going to go back to the old format," Mark told them. "Simon wants the old mix of shots — more audience and guests." The camera people nodded. Sheilah busied herself with the program sheets, aware that her cheeks were flaming from anger.

After the segment was taped, she went to Simon's office. There was no way to avoid him today; she had the briefing papers for the next month and she had to review them with him. Last night, as she thought about Simon, she had made up her mind that she would keep their relationship on a professional level and keep him at a personal distance.

He was working at his desk, his head down, concentrating on writing some questions for a guest.

"If you'll give me a minute of your time and look at this, we'll be ahead of the game," she said, putting the papers on his desk.

"Okay, just a second." He continued writing. "Sit a minute." He indicated a chair. "I want to talk to you too." He put down his pen and then shook his head. "What's gotten into us? We're acting crazy again. It's California all over."

She licked her dry lips before she spoke. "Simon, I told you long ago to forget California and us. That doesn't matter anymore. All that matters is that I'm here to produce this show. Isn't that what you wanted when you pushed me into this job? To help you get good ratings?"

He leaned back in his chair, and she could see the smoldering anger in his eyes. "Oh, no, lady, I didn't push you into this job. You could have refused it. No one twisted your arm."

"That's not the way it was presented to me. You went over my head before I even had a chance to consider it. I was doing quite well where I was." She folded her arms in front of her. "Well, I may have taken this job over my better judgment. I may not be happy with the way I got it — the way you butted into my career — but you were the one who wanted me on your show. You said you needed me. For what? To be a yes-person? To follow you around again?"

"No, of course not. I wanted you here because you're right for the job. This is where you belong."

"Oh, and now you're telling me where I should be in my career? Who says I wanted this job?"

He stared at her, and she could see a vein in his temple throb with anger. "You wanted it, lady," he said roughly. "That's why you took it."

"I took it to help you out."

His voice was clipped. "You took it because you knew it was a step up for you." He stood up and paced around the room. "Listen, Sheilah, you'd have to go far and wide to, quote, help me out, unquote. Don't forget, babe, my show's been top-rated for the past two years."

"Too bad you aren't." She threw her head back and looked at him through narrowed eyes.

"Oh? Really? Let's see how you do in the emotion ratings, honey." He pulled her to him and pressed his lips to hers, and her smoldering anger finally burst into flame. His intrusion into all phases of her life overwhelmed her with resentment, and in a symbolic move of both show and strength she put her hands on his chest, forcing him away. To her surprise he responded by releasing her immediately.

"You lose, sweetheart," he said, sitting down again and speaking in a deadly controlled voice. "You don't even get a share of the ratings. Go find someone else to edit your material — you need it."

Hot tears of rage and humiliation stung at her eyes, and she turned to leave the room, furious and unable to reply to his taunts.

"Go ahead, run away again!" he shouted. "That's your mode of operation, Sheilah. One thing wrong, and you don't stand and fight it out — you'd rather leave. You ran out on me once before."

She stopped and faced him, enraged, yet relieved that the argument was finally out in the open.

"You're darn right I ran out on you before. Don't forget you were the one who forced me to do it." She clenched her fists. "You were so caught up with yourself and your good times — just like now. Oh, sure, I feel something for you — I admit it. I can't help that. I was in love with you once, foolish as it was, and I made no secret about it. But I won't get into that trap again, Simon." She slammed the door, but she could still hear his voice from the outer office.

"That's fine with me, Sheilah. From now on, it's strictly business."

"Which is the way I've always wanted it." She slammed the outer door, oblivious to the harsh sound it made as it reverberated down the corridor and into other offices on the floor.

They were polite when they met in the

studio the next day. She spoke to him only when necessary, and during the break she had Mark ask him to turn toward the camera for a better shot of his profile. He refused, and Sheilah decided not to press the issue.

During the second commercial she again had Mark ask him to turn, but again he declined to follow the suggestion, and she knew that everyone in the booth was now aware of the friction between the two of them. She made no other comments to Simon during the final fifteen minutes, and she was relieved when the credits crawled across the screen.

"That's a wrap," Mark said to no one in particular. "Another fun-filled day, ladies and gents." He touched Sheilah's arm. "Switch on your mike, will you? Simon's signaling he wants to say something."

She clicked the button. "Yes?"

"I told you I don't like profiles."

"We wanted only one or two. I thought it would balance some of the other shots." Her voice was steady, matter-of-fact.

"I don't like those shots, and I asked you to get more audience reaction."

She picked up the mike and raised it close to her lips. "I know you're the star, Simon, but I am the producer. At least that's what my contract says."

Mark turned his head briefly at her words, and she realized that most of the crew members were still either on the set or in the booth and were unable to avoid hearing the conversation.

"Oh, come off it, Sheilah!" Simon shot back. "Give me a break." He pushed back his own mike so that she could see his lips move and yet still hear the amplification of his voice. "Maybe what you need is to really say what's on your mind and stop using my broadcast as a jumping-off place for your problems — whatever they may be."

She saw two crew members look up from the back of the set, startled at Simon's tone, and she knew that everyone was now waiting for her response. She ran her tongue over her dry lips to moisten them and stared silently at Simon through the booth window, trying to forestall the confrontation.

"What's the matter?" he goaded. "Say it. You've been saying this is my program and you don't have any voice in it. Well, this show is all yours." He pushed back his chair from the table and draped his arm over the back of it, and he seemed relaxed, almost as if he were lounging, except for the harshness in his voice, which betrayed him. "You tell me the next line in this script."

She swallowed twice, and then uncontrollable anger welled up within her and she switched the button once again so that her voice could be heard throughout the studio.

"This is a private argument, folks," she said in a steady voice to the crew, "and I'd appreciate it if you would all clear out." She kept her eyes fixed on Simon, and she heard shuffling behind her as Mark and the other people in the control room rolled back their chairs. When she heard the door close, she knew she was alone in the booth. Out of the corner of her eye she could see that the floor technicians had all abandoned their gear and that, finally, she and Simon were the only two people in Studio B.

She continued staring at him, watching as his hand played with the microphone, his finger tapping the speaker in a maddeningly rhythmic beat. She wanted to shout out to him to stop. Her head pounded so that each tap seemed to drive further and further into the top of her skull, and she closed her eyes briefly in an effort to free her from the pain. Somehow, she'd always known it would come to this.

"It's only you and me now, Sheilah, and it's your move," he said, nodding to her slightly. "Say what you have to say. You've been wanting to ever since I came on board this station." His voice was icy, and she shivered as the sound penetrated through her.

Her finger scratched the back of the mike. "Okay," she said, "you want to know why I'm upset? I'm not happy in this job. It's because of you that I'm here — you sweet-talked me into it. But you don't let me work — you don't give me a free hand. You've made changes whenever you've felt like it. You tell people how to handle their jobs. You undermine me at every point. What did you need me for?"

His hand hit the desk in front of the mike so that the sound echoed throughout the empty studio. "Look, ever since I got here you've been making sarcastic remarks, goading me into arguments. But you're right — maybe you shouldn't have taken this job. Maybe we really can't work together." He looked up at her through the glass, and she saw that his jaw was tightening just as she remembered it used to when they were in California and their romance was getting rocky.

She pressed at her forehead. "You're not used to relinquishing any authority. You want — you *need* — total control over everything. Your ego gets in the way all the time, Simon. Just like in California."

"My ego has nothing to do with this, and

you know it. But you're right — it is like California. You're finally getting close to the problem," he said, still toying with the mike. "Close, but no cigar. Now how about some honesty? How about your admitting that there's something else going on in our lives that has a bearing on all this — that we both know we're still attracted to each other — that maybe we should try a little harder to understand what's happening now and forget about the past?"

"No, Simon," she answered, refusing to admit the wisdom of his words, "I'm not about to play 'pick up the pieces' with you. It wouldn't work. And, yes, I am still attracted to you, but I don't want you anymore. It was too difficult loving you. Especially the getting-over-you part — that was hard and hurtful, and I don't want to repeat that lesson ever again."

Simon looked at her, and all traces of his anger seemed to be gone. "No second chances?" he asked in a gentler tone.

"None."

"Okay, we'll play it by your rules." He touched his forehead in a parting salute, and on his way out of the studio he switched off the lights. Sheilah sat there, clicking the control buttons on and off, listening to his footsteps echo throughout the darkened studio until he was finally gone.

"Darn you, Simon!" she said aloud. "Darn you for coming out here, and for ruining my good life, and for putting me into this position and — and —" Her voice faltered. "And for realizing that the show isn't the real reason we're fighting."

She laid her head on the desk, knowing that Simon had spoken the truth — that their past was getting in the way of the present and future.

Finally she sat up and acknowledged the real problem: "You know, don't you, Simon?" she whispered. "You know I'm still in love with you. That I've never really gotten over you." She slowly shook her head, trying to deny the honesty of her statement, and it wasn't until the cleaning woman entered the studio and began to collect the used styrofoam coffee cups that Sheilah realized the time. She switched off the mike, and at the sound the cleaning woman looked up.

"Oh, it's you, Ms. Godfrey. You startled me."

She blinked as the woman turned on the lights. "I guess it's late, Annie," she said, forcing a smile. "Time for me to go home."

"It's only noon, Ms. Godfrey."

"Still, it's late for me."

Long into the night, after all the lights in the adjoining apartment buildings were turned off, Sheilah sat at the darkened window, still thinking about the encounter with Simon.

Okay, she said to herself. *Now what? Where do you go from here? It's all out in the open. What happens now?* She sunk back into the soft pillows of the velour chair, moving slightly so that Gatsby could jump onto her lap and be stroked. She saw the glow of the streetlights below her window and watched idly as a taxicab stopped at her corner and picked up a passenger. She allowed the little street drama to occupy her entire mind, as though thinking about something else would give her the answers to her questions.

"Simon Kent . . . Simon Kent . . . Simon Kent . . ." She said his name over and over again. "It's your move," he had said. She shivered and pulled her robe tighter around her. "You're right, Simon, it *is* my move. But for once in my life I'm not sure which way to go," she said aloud.

CHAPTER FIFTEEN

Beth brought in the morning newspapers and put them on Sheilah's desk, avoiding looking at her.

"It's all right, Beth, I expect it's all over the station by now."

"People always talk, Sheilah."

"I know, but it's what they say that matters, isn't it?"

The phone rang, and Sheilah picked it up.

"I think you need a friend."

"You heard about the blowup, Ben?"

"Hasn't everyone?"

"Thanks, you made my day."

"Come on, Sheilah, you know how fast things travel. You and Simon getting into a shouting match is exactly the sort of thing that makes the rounds quickly. Come on up and I'll give you a cup of coffee and we'll talk about it. I told you I'm a good listener."

Ben sat in his chair across from her, listening intently as she described the scene the previous day.

"So what really caused it?" he asked.

"Lots of things. I'm not sure I like the job. I'm not sure I like working with Simon.

Maybe I shouldn't have taken it."

"You know better than that. It's a good break for you."

"That's just it, Ben. It's as though I'm getting ahead because of Simon."

"That's stretching it a bit."

"No. When we — Simon and I — were out in California, I had the same feeling. I thought I couldn't get ahead unless Simon was helping me."

"This is a little different, isn't it? You didn't get this job because you were Simon's friend."

"Didn't I? Wasn't he the one who suggested me to Mac? Ben, for heaven's sake, it's like he's pulling the strings again for me — like I'm some kind of a puppet."

"That's a little harsh on you, isn't it? You got this job because Mac and the rest of the people here thought you deserved it. You've got enormous talent. Where else could you have gone at this station?"

"Maybe to a new show. A different format — one that I created — I don't know." She slapped the table hard. "Look, Ben, I've never asked for anything except what I deserved."

"And you deserved to produce Simon's show."

She smiled as Ben winced. "That's exactly

what I mean. You called it Simon's show. It would never be considered my show."

"The producer rarely gets credit — except on the titles. Frankly, it'll always be Simon's show. The on-camera personality gets the credit from the viewer — and if the show bombs, the on-camera personality gets the boos. You know that. That's the way it is in TV."

"Yeah, I know."

"But that wasn't the real reason for the blowup, was it?" He smiled. "Sheilah, this is Ben, remember? You and I had a conversation once."

"I remember."

"Isn't that what this is all about?"

"No."

"No? You answered that pretty quickly. Look, I know and you know that you still have a tremendous amount of leftover feelings for Simon. Stuff you never resolved. I think it's about time for you to be honest with yourself."

She pushed the hair away from her forehead. "Tell me how you and Ginger handle your careers."

"Easily — and with lots of work."

"Aren't you afraid that her career might overshadow yours?"

"Sure."

"Doesn't it bother you?"

"Yes, but there's nothing I can do about that. She's in a glamorous career where there's lots of exposure — people see her, know her name. Women want to emulate her — and men want to date her. That's a given. My career is nowhere as exciting, although it's exciting to me. I like what I do but, more important, I'm comfortable in what I do. I know I'm a good personnel director — a good manager and administrator. That's my job, and I'm secure in it."

He pushed his chair away from his desk and stood up. "Look," he said, tapping his foot on the floor, "I can't dance a step. And my singing's worse, so don't ask me to entertain you. But then again, Ginger's a lousy administrator and can't write a memo to save her life." He sat down again, and Sheilah laughed, feeling some of the tension ease from her body.

"Do you see what I'm trying to tell you? If you're good at your job, you make your own name in your own field."

"But Simon and I are in the same field."

"Ah-ha, now you've finally admitted it. It's two-fold, isn't it? You and Simon, personal relationship. And you and Simon, professional relationship. That's what this is all about."

"Yes."

"You're in love with him, aren't you?"

She shrugged, not wanting to admit in words what she now believed. "That's what's so baffling. I really thought I'd left Simon and our relationship back in California. But now all of a sudden he's here, and all those feelings are back too." She rested her head on her hand. "And all it does is confuse me."

"How does Simon feel?"

"He says he wants to just let whatever happens happen."

"Sounds good to me."

"But —"

"But you're afraid to act — or react. You're caught in a bind, aren't you? Why don't you keep your options open? Don't be afraid. You can always pull back."

"But —" she began again.

"I know what you're going to say — that you've already had one go-round. Well, maybe you two need a second chance. If you really want my opinion, Sheilah, I think you should talk to Simon. Tell him how you feel and what you're afraid of, and then see what he has to offer. So what if you're vulnerable? That's what makes people human." He smiled at her. "I sure would hate to think that because I was scared I could miss something wonderful. Think about it."

"I will. Thanks, Ben."

"That's what friends are for."

A few minutes later she sat in her office staring at the phone. She picked it up, replaced it in its cradle, touched it, played with the dial, and then finally picked up the phone again, punched a few numbers, and waited.

"Simon Kent." She swallowed hard and closed her eyes. He repeated his name. "Simon Kent."

She spoke very quietly into the mouthpiece. "Can we talk?"

There was a brief pause. "Sure. Now?"

"Yes," she said quickly.

"Okay. Your place or mine?" When she didn't answer, he added, "Oh, heck, it doesn't matter. I'll be there in fifteen minutes."

She exhaled, walked around the room, looked at her own reflection in the small mirror hanging next to the door, rubbed at her cheeks, and then sat down again and waited for him.

He came into her office and closed the door behind him. He was wearing an old sweater that she recognized from before, and she looked away, trying to forget forbidden memories and feelings she was still trying to deny in words. She saw when he turned full face to her that there were little dark lines around his eyes that she had never noticed before. She had a momentary shock that five years had indeed passed since they were together.

"I thought it might be better if we say what we have to in private," he said, and she nodded her head, agreeing with him. "It's still your move. What's on your mind?" He seemed relaxed, but she recognized the signs that indicated his anger: the up-and-down stretching of his fingers on the chair arms as though he were playing an imaginary piano; the cold, penetrating gaze that seemed to go through and past her; the almost totally immobile face trained on hers.

"Need help?" His voice was calm, unwavering.

She half folded her hands on the desk top, unconsciously flicking her thumb with her ring finger.

"You still do it, don't you?" His eyes briefly went first to her fingers and then to her face, and she saw an almost imperceptible half smile of either remembrance or regret. She wondered which one he was feeling.

"Old habits are hard to lose."

"Which brings us around to the reason

why I'm here." He walked to the window and looked out to the pale, bleak, cloudy sky. "Let's get on with this. We still have a show to put on in a couple of hours, remember?"

"I owe you an apology," she blurted out.

"You bet you do!" he exploded, and she half jumped at the loudness of it.

"You have a right to be angry, but I think I was justified too."

"Look, hold it right there." His back was silhouetted against the window, and as she watched him she saw small snowflakes begin to trickle down from the sky. "You've been riding me much too long. I don't mind if you and I have a disagreement about policy or production or guests or whatever, but that's not the real reason you've been on my back, and that's what we have to talk about." He ran his hand through his hair. "We've got to clear up some things."

"Yes, but first my job. There's something wrong."

"What?"

She folded her hands. "I'm not producing anything meaningful. That's what I miss. Darn it, Simon, if you didn't want to use my skills, why did you box me into this job?"

"We've had conferences."

"Sure, but those conferences always end with what you want, and there have been times when I've walked away from them convinced that I just caved in to satisfy you."

"You what?" The words were punctuated slowly, bitingly.

"When I give an order, you rescind it. When I think a certain shot would make it visually interesting, you countermand it. When I do anything, you go over my head. Don't you see, it's the same old story again and again and again!" She swallowed hard. "I just don't get the feeling that I'm producing this show. I get the feeling that you're the head honcho and that you always will be and that no matter what I do it's never going to work."

He inhaled deeply, and she could see his fingers begin a silent symphony in the air as he began to pace the room in large strides. As she watched she began to recall some of the reasons why she was first attracted to him in California.

There are some things, Simon, she thought, *that I guess I'll never forget. The way you used to walk around the room when you were thinking . . . and the way your eyes had that faraway look when you tried to resolve something. I don't think I'll ever forget those looks.*

She blinked, calling herself back from her memories.

"You may be right," he said. He relaxed and smiled slightly. "I'm not totally egotistical. And I know I do press my points defensively."

"Uh-huh."

"But, Sheilah, if you felt that strongly about some things, why didn't you fight for them? You never had any trouble when we were in California. When I think of those shouting matches we had. . . ."

"I got tired of the shouting. We both did."

He whistled softly. "I guess so. What can I say to you to make you believe that I wanted you on the show? I admired your work. And I truly thought the change would be good for everyone. It had nothing to do with whether I still love you or not."

"Do you?" She was surprised at how easily she asked the question.

"I think so." He touched her shoulder as he paced close to her. "I'd like to find out for sure . . . we've both changed."

"We have."

He sighed and held out his hand. "We'll discuss the ideas more rationally and all decisions will be made jointly. Now, what about us?"

"Let's just see what happens."

"That's all I ask." He tightened his grip on her hand, squeezing it, and she was amazed at how quickly her anger disappeared. "Now, come on," he said, "we've got a show to do."

The set was unusually quiet when she entered the booth and switched on her mike and tested it. She saw that everyone was avoiding looking at her while they went through the formalities of readying the studio for the morning's broadcast; the usual bantering and joking among the crew members was absent. She paused and then flipped the switch once more.

"I know you're all extra-busy today," she began, "and that industry is partly my fault, so if you'll all either pay attention or look at me and pretend you are, I'd like to apologize for my outburst yesterday. It shouldn't have happened — it wasn't anyone's fault, and above all, it was unprofessional. I'm sorry."

"Takes two to argue," she heard Simon say over the loudspeakers. "So what Sheilah said goes double. It won't happen again, and if anyone ever tries it, including me, you're off the show." There was silence, and he added, "Of course, ladies and gentlemen, if I'm off the show, you'd better polish up your résumés." There was a ripple of laughter as everyone relaxed and began to joke once more and Simon mingled with the crew.

Why is it, Simon, she thought, looking into the monitor at him, *that you're able to detonate a sticky situation so easily? And what makes me want to run — not run . . . laugh . . . cry, and even think about seriously trying to catch the brass ring with you again?*

CHAPTER SIXTEEN

It was more than the thrill of winning the award, Sheilah thought as she cradled the golden statue in her arms. It was the combination of being recognized by her peers and finally accomplishing what she had set out to achieve when she'd first begun in broadcasting. It had been an evening to remember. Now, looking at Simon as he drove her back to her home after the dinner, she remembered the way he looked as he'd called her name and the way he'd kissed her when he handed her the prize that said much more than the fact that he was glad she was the winner.

She held on to the statue, watching it glint as they passed close to streetlights. She rubbed it as though it were a talisman, as though doing so would preserve the night forever. They were both silent as he guided the car through midtown, and she leaned back into the soft velour of the seat, looking out at the night people and tourists who were walking around Central Park.

"Want a nightcap? To celebrate?" he asked.

"No, I'm absolutely drained."

"It's the aftereffects of winning, of being keyed up." He said it as a matter of fact.

"Does it still happen to you?"

"All the time. Even when I lose." They drove past the theater district, and he gestured toward the marquees. "I used to feel that that's what it would be like to win. Like having my name up in lights for all the world to see."

"They are now. In front of the studio."

He shrugged. "I've gotten used to it. So will you."

She exhaled. "Give me time."

He glanced into the rearview mirror, then pulled around a horse-drawn carriage. "It really means that much to you?"

"Yes."

"Why?"

"Because it means that what I wanted to do — what I was doing — was right."

He nodded. "Do you think you're doing a good job?"

"Sure."

"Then that's how you evaluate it. You don't need anyone to tell you you're good."

"But this — this," she said, holding the gleaming object above her head, "makes it easier for me to produce programs I want on the air."

"So it's a bargaining chip."

"It sure is." She smiled to herself and traced the engraving on the award, letting her gloved finger pause for a moment on her name.

"It's respect — that's what it is." He said it softly, and in the dark enclosed space of the car she thought the word echoed from one side to the other, from the front to the back to the front again. She found herself nodding in agreement.

"It means," she said, looking at him, "that I can finally be my own person."

"You always were." He took his eyes off the lamp-lit street for a second to smile at her. "You know, your winning that makes it easier for me."

"For what?" She frowned, and her shoulders slumped with fatigue.

"I can talk to you now about us. The pressure is finally off you — off us."

"You're taking advantage of the time."

He shook his head, and when he spoke, she heard the honesty in his voice. "I don't want the advantage. What I want, Sheilah, is for us to be together."

"Oh, Simon, we were once, but I took too much for granted and you — you didn't take us seriously enough."

"I learned."

"Too late, though."

He drove past the darkened buildings, past the workers who were repairing the streets. He expertly maneuvered the car between two buses and then moved ahead of them.

"I knew it before, Sheilah. I knew it, but I denied it. We were both too independent then. We both wanted to conquer the world, and neither you nor I wanted anybody's help." He inhaled deeply. "Think about it, Sheilah — didn't we lie a lot? To ourselves — and to each other?"

He stopped for a red light, and the flashing light of a jazz club's neon sign filled the interior of the car with a smoky blue color, and the two of them seemed trapped in an eerie night world until the light changed and he continued down the street.

"Is that what you really want?" she asked, shifting in her seat so that she could see him better.

He was quiet and didn't answer as he pulled into a rare empty space in front of her apartment building. He turned the ignition key off and adjusted the brake, and she could see him concentrating, unaware of doing the necessary mechanical things.

"Is that what I really want?" he finally repeated and again fell silent. She recalled how he always used that tactic of repetition to get at a response that seemed to elude him. She watched a few late-night people cross the street and go into the restaurant on the corner while Simon struggled with the answer to her question.

"Yes," he said finally, and the way he said the one word acknowledged all he was thinking and feeling.

She tilted her head. "Are you sure it's not merely traces of a past romance?"

"It's not." He put his arm around her and pulled her closer to him so that she felt his tweed coat next to her face, and she relaxed within its roughness.

"Sheilah, remember that first night when I came here — when you asked me why I was leaving California, why I would consider coming out here — and I couldn't answer?"

"Uh-huh."

"I know the answer now." His lips brushed her hair. "You. It was always you." He kissed the top of her head. "It's that simple. I guess you were always in my heart even when I wasn't consciously thinking of you — even when I didn't want to think of you."

He tightened his grip around her and gently kissed her forehead. "But there were times when I would see or hear something — maybe I had a guest who bordered on the ridiculous and it reminded me of your crazy sense of humor, or I came across a shade of blue that you used to wear, or I'd see a woman who resembled you from far away — and for a brief moment I would stop and think of you . . . about what you might be doing or about what we once had done together. And I would brood about it. I even debated calling you once or twice."

He kissed the corner of her eye, and she blinked so that her eyelash caressed his lips. "I lied to you — I did have your number, but. . . ." His voice trailed off, and she saw him rub the tiny scar on his cheek. She felt a soft glow surround her and cloud her thoughts.

"Why didn't you?"

"Because I was either too foolish or too insecure or too scared to call you." His mouth gently glided across her cheek. "I was afraid of how you would react. I really thought you didn't want anything to do with me — that I had killed your love. And of course that macho Simon of the old days couldn't take a rejection — not about something as important as that." He kissed her lower lip, and she felt her entire mouth tremble in anticipation. "That's why no one ever measured up to my ideas of love and marriage, and that's one of the reasons I've come here — to reclaim you — to reclaim your love and keep it, if you'll give it to me a second time."

He tilted her face upward to him. "I've always loved you, Sheilah, although, God knows, I fought it. But these past few weeks, being here with you, seeing you — I know, finally, and I can admit it. It's you, Sheilah — I love you." His mouth pressed down on hers, and she reached up, statuette in hand, and pulled him to her, taking an extra gulp of air before kissing him once again.

"Simon," she said at last, "there are so many things I want to do."

"We'll do them together." He smoothed her hair with his chin.

"I mean professionally."

"You can do them." He kissed the top of her head. "You can do anything you want. You don't have to prove anything to anyone now." He pulled her even closer into the circle of his arms, and she felt the glowing feeling completely envelop her as though his arms were a magical fortress that excluded practical thoughts and the rest of the world.

She looked up at him, and even in the dark she saw and remembered the way a lock of his hair fell straight across his forehead whenever it was newly cut. She reached up and touched it, pushing it across the part and making it orderly, and she realized that for the first time since he'd returned she was beginning to merge the old Simon she knew and remembered with the person who was now holding her.

"We are different, aren't we?"

"Older and wiser."

"There will be times when we don't agree. . . ."

"Of course," he said, bending down to kiss her again.

"And we'll talk them out?" She spoke the words quietly, using only a minimum of breath.

"Yes." He tilted her head upward so that his mouth was close to her ear. "Say it, Sheilah — say it," he urged, and she felt the glow deepen and spread over and within her until it seemed to completely surround the both of them. And then softly, very softly, she spoke.

"I love you, Simon. I think I always have. I know I always will. I love you, Simon."

The employees of THORNDIKE PRESS hope you have enjoyed this Large Print book. All our Large Print books are designed for easy reading — and they're made to last.

Other Thorndike Large Print books are available at your library, through selected bookstores, or directly from us. Suggestions for books you would like to see in Large Print are always welcome.

For more information about current and upcoming titles, please call or mail your name and address to:

THORNDIKE PRESS
PO Box 159
Thorndike, Maine 04986
800/223-6121
207/948-2962